THE CROOKED LITTLE PATH

A Book of Nature Stories by
THORNTON W. BURGESS

Illustrated by
HARRISON CADY

BONANZA BOOKS · NEW YORK

This edition published by Bonanza Books,
a division of Crown Publishers, Inc.,
by arrangement with Little, Brown and Company
d e f g h

PRINTED IN THE UNITED STATES OF AMERICA

Contents

THE CROOKED LITTLE PATH

I. The Crooked Little Path

The Path of Life is seldom straight.
Around each turn adventures wait.
— OLD MOTHER NATURE

THE CROOKED LITTLE PATH begins at the edge of the woods and winds among the trees far into the Green Forest to the Great Mountain. It makes sudden bends this way and that way. It twists and turns around stumps and big rocks. It climbs little hills and runs down the other sides. It clambers over old logs and fallen trees. It loafs along the bank of Laughing Brook, then skips across on steppingstones. It squeezes between close-growing trees and hides beneath overhanging ferns. It tries to

3

lose itself in thickets of young evergreens. It grows faint along open stony ridges and recovers in sunny hollows. It wanders over hill and down dale, seemingly without purpose yet always leading from here to there, and it is beloved by all who follow it.

Many feet have made and are still making the Crooked Little Path. Some are big feet. Some are not so big. Some are tiny. Some are padded and soft. Some are hard, sharp-edged, and without toes. Some are horny, having wide-spreading toes. Some have long sharp claws. Some have short stout claws. Some are shod with leather, for the Crooked Little Path is sometimes used by Man.

Some of those many feet move slowly with many stops. Some shuffle. Some bound along with quick jumps, and some hop. Some walk without haste. Some trot lightly. Some run swiftly, and some tiny ones seem to dart along the Crooked Little Path. Some use it daily and some only now and again. Some follow far along its crooked length and some keep to it for but a little way. Some there are that tread it boldly, and some with stealth and secrecy.

Dainty ferns and shy flowers grow beside the Crooked Little Path. Crimson and golden and brown leaves carpet it in autumn, and in winter it becomes a winding ribbon of unbroken smoothness set to record the footprints of those who come and go. Love and fear and hate and dread and joy and thrift and carelessness and greed and hope and happiness and hunger and de-

4

sire and watchfulness and courage pass along the Crooked Little
Path, or pause beside it, or fly above it.

Stout oak trees drop acorns in it, and the sweet three-sided
little beechnuts hide under its carpet of fallen leaves. Madam Orb
the Spider spreads her wondrous net of shining silk across it to
be filled with sun-jeweled drops of dew in the early morning
and later catch a heedless fly. The Black Shadows coming out
from the Purple Hills veil it in soft dusk in the early evening.
Later moonbeams coming down between the treetops search
for it and find it in places to lose it again as clouds bring drifting interference.

The Merry Little Breezes dance along it by day, and after
dark the wandering Little Night Breezes follow it with mes-
sages for furtive folk and timid folk. It holds the secrets of
many in fur and feathers and of some with neither. In summer
it loiters through dusky dells to listen to the matin song of
the Hermit Thrush and the vesper melody of the Wood Thrush.
In winter it holds its way despite the fury of rough Brother
North Wind and the bitter cold of Jack Frost.

It could tell if it would of funny things and wonderful things
and beautiful things and dreadful things that it has known. It
has seen many come and many go, some never to return. It
welcomes the stranger and it speeds him on his way. So the
Crooked Little Path shows the way to all who live in or visit the
Green Forest and is beloved by them.

5

Perhaps that is why Buster Bear, roaming restlessly on the Great Mountain, remembered the Crooked Little Path and wondered if it might lead him to a place he must find soon wherein to sleep through the winter, and started down for that part of the Green Forest through which the Crooked Little Path shows

the way. He had found no place in the Great Mountain to suit him.

Buster has no real home unless you call his winter den where he sleeps through the cold weather his home. In the summer and fall he roams about looking for food and he knows all the best places for long distances round about. None knows better than he where the berries are biggest and sweetest and most plentiful. None knows better than he where acorns and beech-nuts will be most abundant when Jack Frost and the Merry Little Breezes shake them loose to drop and hide under the fallen leaves. Some of these places are very far apart but Buster doesn't mind. He is a great traveler, is Buster Bear. That is why he has no real home.

Sometimes he spends the winter in a neighborhood where he has been all summer. Other times he migrates. To migrate is simply to leave a neighborhood where you have been living to go to another place, usually a long distance away. Buster doesn't go from the Far North to the sunny South like so many of the feathered folk. Of course not. But he does sometimes travel farther than you might think in search of a place in which to spend a comfortable winter.

"Having to go to sleep for the winter is a nuisance. Yes, sir, is a nuisance. I don't like it," grumbled Buster as he way down the Great Mountain.

"Then why do you do it?" ask happened to be near enough

"Because I must or starve to death," growled Buster.

"I don't go to sleep for the winter and I don't starve to death, yet I am bigger than you. If you would eat what I eat you wouldn't have to go to sleep. It is plain, simple food, but there is plenty of it," replied Flathorns.

"I can't; that's why," growled Buster.

"I don't see why not. It is here for the taking," retorted Flathorns. "What is the trouble?"

"Call it stomach trouble, for that is what it is," growled Buster. "I guess our stomachs are different. They must be. I would starve to death on what you eat. Besides, I wouldn't like it. Probably you would starve to death on what I eat and must have. So I guess our stomachs are different" — which was a very good guess on Buster's part.

"So you let your stomach put you to sleep for the winter," grunted Flathorns. "I eat what I like but I don't let my stomach tell me what I shall or shall not eat."

"Huh!" growled Buster Bear. "Do you eat what you don't like?"

"Of course I don't!" snorted Flathorns.

"You don't eat what you don't like and you don't like what ___ stomach can't use, so it *is* your stomach that decides what ___ shall not eat. I guess it is the same way with every-___ ___ you eat and so I have to go to bed when ___ found that I can eat. Then I sleep ___ chance of finding things that my stomach approves," replied Buster in his grumbly, rumbly voice.

"And what is your stomach saying now?" asked Flathorns.

"That I better be looking for more to put in it or else hunt a place to go to sleep, and that is what I am doing," growled Buster. He shuffled along the Crooked Little Path into the Green Forest.

II. Peter Hears a Rumor

Before you put your tongue to use
Be sure you have a real excuse.
— OLD MOTHER NATURE

BUSTER BEAR was back in the Green Forest that spreads far
between the Great Mountain and the Green Meadows and the
Old Pasture. He had been living on the Great Mountain so
long that he had been almost forgotten by the little people of the
Green Forest. Now he was back and the news of his return had
spread among the Green Forest folk in that mysterious way that
is one of Mother Nature's secrets. It seemed as if Buster had

hardly put foot on the Crooked Little Path before all the Green Forest knew of it.

Peter Rabbit heard it from his cousin, Jumper the Hare. They had met just a little way in from the edge. Peter had come over from the dear Old Briar-patch for no good reason at all, although he wouldn't have admitted that. Probably he would have said that important business had brought him there. It is queer how important to oneself a matter of no importance to anyone else can be.

Anyway he was there and the first thing Jumper the Hare said was, "Buster Bear is back."

"Who says so?" asked Peter, looking a little startled.

"All the Green Forest knows it," replied Jumper.

"Have you seen him?" demanded Peter.

"No," admitted Jumper.

"Have you seen anybody who has seen him?" persisted Peter.

"No," replied Jumper.

"Have you seen his footprints, or do you know anyone who has?" demanded Peter.

Again Jumper had to give the same answer, "No."

"Then you don't *know* he is back," declared Peter.

"Everybody in the Green Forest knows it," retorted Jumper sharply. "If you don't believe it ask anyone else you chance to meet. They'll tell you it is true."

"I believe you think it is true, Cousin Jumper, but that doesn't make it true. You haven't seen Buster Bear or any signs of him and you don't know anyone who has. You have merely *heard* that Buster is back. That is just rumor. It is foolish to be sure a rumor is the truth," said Peter mildly.

"And it may be dangerous not to," retorted his big cousin. "Truth or just rumor, I am going to watch for Buster Bear. He isn't going to catch me. If you have any sense at all, Cousin Peter, you will go back to the dear Old Briar-patch where you belong. Buster Bear isn't likely to go over there, but there is no knowing when you may meet him here."

Of course that was sound advice, but of course it was wasted, as sound advice so often is. Peter parted from his cousin and started along the Crooked Little Path. He didn't run in his usual heedless way, lipperty, lipperty, lip. He hopped slowly, stopping often to look and listen, all the time feeling a pleasant tingle of excitement. It might be only a rumor that Buster Bear was back in the Green Forest. He believed it was. But it might be true. He wanted to know which it was. He just couldn't go back home without finding out or at least trying to.

At a turn in the Crooked Little Path he met Prickly Porky the Porcupine shuffling along and complaining of nothing in particular and everything in general. He had no cause to complain. It was a form of pleasure. Yes, sir, complaining was a sort of pleasure. Some people are like that. Peter politely stepped aside. Prickly Porky stopped to scratch his nose.

"I hear Buster Bear is back," said Peter.

"Yes, he is back. He should have stayed on the Great Mountain where he belongs. He is just one more nuisance around here," complained Prickly Porky.

"Have you seen him?" asked Peter.

"No," grunted Prickly Porky.

"Then how do you know he is back?" Peter demanded.

"Everybody says so, so it must be so," grunted Prickly Porky. Walking over to a tree he began to climb it.

So it went. Everyone Peter met said Buster was back yet no one had seen him.

Peter went home, but he couldn't forget what he had heard. "Everybody says that Buster Bear is back in the Green Forest," said he to Mrs. Peter.

"Then it must be so," Mrs. Peter replied and added, "I hope that now you will have sense enough to stay at home."

Peter pretended not to have heard that last. "Everybody saying a thing is so doesn't make it so. It can be just a rumor," said Peter.

"Rumor or fact I hope now you will keep out of the Green Forest," retorted Mrs. Peter.

"But if I don't go over there how am I to find out if it is true?" asked Peter.

"What difference does it make to you?" snapped Mrs. Peter rather crossly. She was beginning to lose patience.

"But I have to know," persisted Peter.

"You don't have to know and you know you don't have to know. It is just curiosity," retorted Mrs. Peter.

Peter changed the subject and at the first opportunity slipped out of the dear Old Briar-patch and headed for the Green Forest, lipperty, lipperty, lip. "I do have to know," said Peter to himself. "I can't help thinking about it and wondering about it until I know." Curiosity is like that.

So once more Peter hopped along the Crooked Little Path all eyes and ears. The first person he saw was Whitefoot the Wood Mouse. As usual Whitefoot looked ready to run at no more than the rustle of a falling leaf.

"What are you doing over here? Don't you know that Buster Bear is back in the Green Forest?" squeaked Whitefoot. He looked all about anxiously.

"Have you seen him?" asked Peter eagerly.

"No," squeaked Whitefoot. "No, I haven't seen him and I don't want to see him. It is enough for me to know that he is around."

Before Peter could ask how he knew Whitefoot darted out of sight. "He doesn't *know* any more than I do," muttered Peter and moved on.

Presently he saw Mrs. Grouse ahead of him in the Crooked Little Path. He hurried to catch up with her for they are old friends. Mrs. Grouse saw him coming and waited for him.

"Why the hurry, Peter Rabbit? Is Buster Bear after you?" she asked.

"Then Buster Bear really is back in the Green Forest!" cried Peter eagerly.

"So they say," replied Mrs. Grouse.

Peter's face fell. "Is that all you know about it?" he asked.

Mrs. Grouse nodded. "Isn't that enough? It is for me," said she.

"But you haven't seen him or signs of him or anyone who has seen him, so you can't really *know*," cried Peter. "I should think you would look for him and so make sure," he added.

"Listen, Peter: I know enough to know that trouble comes without being looked for. If Buster Bear doesn't bother me I don't care whether he is in the Green Forest or not. If he comes my way I'll see him because I'll be watching for him. If he isn't in the Green Forest I'll lose nothing because of a little extra watchfulness. What Buster Bear does, or where he is, is no business of mine as long as he leaves me alone," replied Mrs. Grouse tartly.

Peter sighed. "I wish I could really know," said he wistfully.

"Do you know the surest and quickest way of getting into trouble?" asked Mrs. Grouse, her black eyes twinkling.

"No. What is?" replied Peter innocently.

"Having too much curiosity," said Mrs. Grouse. Spreading her stout wings she whirred away.

III. The Footprint

Careless feet will leave behind
Records other people find.
— OLD MOTHER NATURE

FOOTPRINTS are important. They tell tales. They give away
secrets. They are a record of wandering feet, careless feet, sly
feet, eager feet, cruel feet, curious feet, brave feet, cowardly
feet, kindly feet, loving feet. It has been so ever since the world
was young. It is so today. The wise watch their steps.

Peter Rabbit was following the Crooked Little Path deep in
the Green Forest, deeper than he ever had ventured before. Perhaps he didn't realize how far he had come. It was easy to travel

16

in the Crooked Little Path and it was very pleasant. Also it was exciting. There was no knowing what or who might be around the next turn, and somehow there was always a next turn in sight just a little way ahead. Peter just *had* to peek around it. So he was led deeper and deeper into the Green Forest.

But it wasn't just the Crooked Little Path that was leading him on. No, sir, it wasn't just that. It was another kind of curiosity. He wanted to *know* if it was true that Buster Bear was back in the Green Forest. So he kept on along the Crooked Little Path farther and farther into the Green Forest, asking all he met if they really knew that Buster Bear was back. Not one of them doubted that he was but not one *knew* that he was. Peter began really to doubt. The more he doubted the greater became the urge to keep on to make sure one way or the other.

"It is just a rumor now. A rumor may be true or it may be false. It should be proved true before it is believed. Rumors that are not true can do a lot of harm. If Buster Bear isn't back a lot of people are excited over nothing and some of them are worrying without cause. Goodness knows we Green Forest and Green Meadow folks have enough reasons to worry without being caused needless worry. Folks should be careful about starting rumors. Perhaps someone thought he saw Buster Bear and didn't wait to find out if he really did before starting the rumor. I think that is just what happened. I don't believe Buster Bear is back in the Green Forest." So thought Peter as he came to where the

Crooked Little Path loafed along the bank of Laughing Brook for a short distance.

Peter sat down on the bank. Never having been as far up Laughing Brook as this he wondered if some of his friends had, Jerry Muskrat for one.

"Of course Little Joe Otter has. He is a great traveler. And I guess perhaps Billy Mink has. He does a lot of traveling too," said Peter, talking to himself. "I wonder how far the Crooked Little Path follows Laughing Brook. I suppose I ought to turn back. Mrs. Peter would say I am crazy to have come so far, but she thinks I am crazy if I leave the dear Old Briar-patch at all. I'll go just a little farther. I would like to know how far the Crooked Little Path and Laughing Brook stay together."

So Peter started on. Soon he came to where the Crooked Little Path crossed Laughing Brook on steppingstones and then wandered on out of sight around a turn. The steppingstones were big and flat. He sat down and stared across and wondered what it was like around that turn on the other side. He could cross on those steppingstones and find out. He looked at them to see how far apart they were and for the first time noticed that they were wet in places although they were above water. And then he saw something that sent such cold chills over him that he couldn't move. It was as if he was all in an instant frozen right there. In the mud right in front of him was a footprint freshly made, the biggest footprint he ever had seen. Someone had just

18

come across on those steppingstones, someone whose feet were wet.

Peter stared at that footprint until it seemed as if his eyes must pop right out of his head. Then somewhere near, seemingly back of him, there was a rustling of dry leaves. It was a very faint rustle. It might have been made by the passing of a Merry Little Breeze. It might have been made by small feet scurrying over the dry leaves on the ground. It might have been made by a big foot, the foot that had made that print in the mud.

Peter didn't wait to find out which it was. It was as if that faint sound had released a spring under him, sending him flying through the air in a long jump. He landed with a splash in shallow water, for he had been facing Laughing Brook. Just how he got across he didn't know, but he did get across and in a hurry too. Then away he ran from the Crooked Little Path and under the thickest brush he could find. He dodged this way. He dodged that way. He ran just as he would have run had Reddy Fox or Old Man Coyote been right at his heels. He didn't stop until he had to to get his breath and rest. He just couldn't run any more right then.

Wet, tired and out of breath he squatted under a little hemlock tree. He had turned to face the way he had come. His long ears were set to catch every sound however faint and his eyes were wide with fright as he peered from his hiding place. From far off came faintly the harsh voice of Croaker the Raven. This

19

was the only sound. No one was after him. He sat there a long time. Sure that he wasn't being chased, that no one was looking for him, he was no longer afraid. Like so many others of the little people of the Green Forest and the Green Meadows Peter is easily frightened and recovers from fright as easily.

Presently he ventured out from his hiding place. Then he made a discovery. He was lost. Yes, sir, he was lost. He didn't know which way to go. He hadn't the least idea where he was excepting that he was deep in the Green Forest where he never had been before. He had run so far and had dodged this way and that so much that he didn't know which way to turn to find the Crooked Little Path or Laughing Brook.

It was disturbing. It was upsetting. How was he ever to get back to the dear Old Briar-patch? Then he remembered something that right away made him feel better.

"Anyway I know now," said he happily, speaking aloud because he thought no one was near.

"What do you know?" asked a small squeaky voice.

Peter looked all around for the speaker. Finally he discovered a pair of bright small eyes watching him. A Wood Mouse was sitting on an old stump close by. "I know that Buster Bear really has come back to the Green Forest," replied Peter.

"Have you seen him?" squeaked the Mouse.

"No," replied Peter.

"Do you know anyone who has seen him?" squeaked the Mouse.

"No," replied Peter, "but —"

"Then you don't *know*," squeaked the other.

"I do so!" retorted Peter a bit sharply.

"How do you know?" the Mouse squeaked just as sharply.

"I have seen his footprint. That's how I know. And you know as well as I do that there is no other footprint that can possibly be mistaken for one of his," replied Peter.

21

IV. An Open Secret

A secret may be secret still
Though anyone may see who will.
— OLD MOTHER NATURE

YOU SEE PEOPLE doing things that you do not understand, or that to you seem foolish or silly, and you wonder if they know what they are about. It may be sometimes that they don't, but as a rule they do.

Peter Rabbit was startled by strange sounds ahead of him and a little to one side of the direction in which he was headed. At first they were faint in the distance. Peter sat up to listen. He can listen better sitting up. Anyway he seems to think he can. He listened for a long time. At first he was frightened. That was because he was in a strange place and those were strange sounds. Then he became curious. The longer he sat the less frightened he was and the more curious he grew. In that Peter was being himself.

He hopped a little way straight toward those sounds and sat up again. He could hear them plainer now but he was no wiser than before as to who or what was making them. He was more curious than ever. Of course. He wouldn't have been Peter if he had not been. He moved a little nearer. The sounds were louder and clearer. His curiosity was greater. Some of the sounds were grunts. He was sure of that. Some seemed like whines. He wasn't sure about those. And some were the cracking of breaking branches. He moved a little nearer and there was the blessed Crooked Little Path! Those sounds came from a hollow on the other side of it.

Peter forgot to be afraid. Yes, sir, he did so. Curiosity can do that. It can make one forget everything but its own desire to be gratified. That is when it may become dangerous. Curiosity out of control cannot be trusted and so always is dangerous.

Peter could see a thicket of young hemlock trees. They were small trees growing very close together, too close for all of them ever to become fine big trees. As they grew some would be crowded to death by stronger neighbors until at last only a few of the strongest would be left to keep on growing into fine big trees. But just now those little hemlock trees were green and just beginning to crowd each other.

Some of those sounds came from the middle of that thicket. Again they seemed to come from beyond that thicket as if the maker of them had left it and was outside. The little trees were too tall for Peter to see over them and too close together for him to see between them. And he *had* to see. Of course. Wouldn't you have *had* to see had you been in his place?

Little by little he moved around until he was where he could see the other side of that thicket. At first no one was to be seen. A moment later a big black head was poked out of the thicket. Peter felt the same chilly feeling that had possessed him when he had discovered that big footprint in the mud by Laughing Brook. He held his breath and watched the maker of that footprint come out of the thicket. It was Buster Bear!

Buster didn't even look in Peter's direction. He shuffled over to a hemlock tree with branches growing nearly to the ground. Peter could see the white stubs of branches that had been broken off. At first he didn't notice them, but when he saw Buster Bear break off another he did notice them and guessed right away that Buster had broken off other branches.

Buster dragged the branch into the thicket. Peter could hear him dragging it about and grumbling in a voice that was half growl, half whine. Now was Peter's chance to get away from there unseen. He turned to do this. He took one hop, then stopped. Curiosity was at work again. That was a queer thing for Buster Bear to be doing. What was he about?

"I wonder," said Peter to himself, but he was careful not to say it aloud. Then he settled himself to watch.

There are many open secrets along the Crooked Little Path. Things right in plain sight are unseen by those who pass. Sometimes they are unseen because they are too plainly in sight to be seen. That doesn't make sense, does it? But it is true. If you get well enough acquainted with Old Mother Nature she will show you many such secrets. Many of her children often hide right in plain sight. They can do it because people do not see what they are not expecting to see, or hoping to see, and few expect or hope to see a secret right in plain sight. That is the kind of secret an open secret is, a secret that anyone can know but few do know.

Would you think that anyone as big as Buster Bear could have an open secret? Of course you wouldn't. Nobody would. Anyway very few would. Had anyone told Peter Rabbit that great big Buster could have such a secret he would have said that such talk was simply foolish. Yet here he was discovering for himself just such a secret. However, he didn't know it yet.

Now and then Buster came out of the thicket, shuffled over to the hemlock tree and broke off a bough. This he would drag or carry back into the thicket and there fuss for a while. About the time Peter would feel that he couldn't possibly sit still another minute but must somehow creep into that thicket and find out what Buster was about Buster would come out for another bough.

Peter forgot something. He forgot to be afraid. Sometimes it it a good thing to forget to be afraid. It always is when fears are needless. As a rule, however, one should never forget to be afraid unless sure no danger is near. But Peter forgot. Curiosity made him. Yes, sir, curiosity made Peter forget. It does that to people. It is one of the bad things about curiosity. A lot of people have lost their lives and still more have been badly hurt just because curiosity led them to forget to watch for danger.

Peter took a hop nearer to the place where Buster Bear went in and out of the thicket. He sat still as long as he could. Buster came out and went back in. He didn't see Peter. He was too intent on what he was doing even to look around. No, Buster Bear wasn't careless. Being so big he didn't need to be watchful. He wasn't afraid of anybody but hunters with dreadful guns, and he was sure that none was in that part of the Green Forest.

Peter hopped a good long hop nearer the entrance. I suspect he wasn't even aware that he had taken that hop. He sat still as long as he could, then hopped again. Finally he was so near the passage Buster Bear had made that one more good hop would put him where he could poke his head around the corner and look right into the middle of the thicket. He waited until Buster was well inside dragging another bough, then took that hop and eagerly peered inside.

What he expected to see I don't know but what he did see was a partly made bed of green boughs and Buster fussing with the bough he had just brought in trying to place it to suit him. Peter had found an open secret, the place where Buster Bear would sleep through the winter, but he didn't know it. Perhaps Buster didn't really know it himself.

V. Buster Bear Turns In

The truth you're sure of as you see it
May sometimes happen not to be it.

— BUSTER BEAR

OF COURSE what Buster Bear was doing was no business of Peter's, but Peter gave no thought to that. He was curious, very, very curious, and when did curiosity ever bother about what is or is not its business? He *had* to know what Buster was about. So Peter just hung around. He couldn't tear himself away.

Whisky Jack the Canada Jay, own cousin to Sammy Jay, spied Peter. "Hi, Longears! What are you doing so far from home?" asked Whisky Jack.

Peter paid no attention to the question. "Do you see what Buster Bear is doing?" Peter asked excitedly.

"Of course I see what he is doing. There is nothing the matter with my eyes," retorted Whisky Jack.

"Well, what is he doing?" demanded Peter impatiently.

"He is making a bed," was the prompt reply.

"What for?" asked Peter.

"To sleep on of course. What are beds usually made for?" retorted Whisky Jack testily.

"But what a lot of work just for a nap!" exclaimed Peter.

"Who said anything about a nap?" demanded Whisky Jack.

"You did. You said he is making a bed to sleep on," retorted Peter.

"So I did, but I didn't say anything about a nap. While I haven't asked him, it being none of my business, I have an idea Buster Bear is getting ready for winter," replied Whisky Jack.

"Don't be silly!" exclaimed Peter.

"Who says I'm silly?" demanded Whisky Jack sharply.

"I do," said Peter. "You know as well as I do that Buster Bear sleeps most of the winter and anyone who sleeps like that has to be under cover. Buster sleeps in a cave, or under a big pile of fallen trees, or in some such place. Everybody knows that."

"You know a lot, don't you? Well, you still have some things to learn, Peter Rabbit. You still have some things to learn. Why don't you ask Buster Bear what he is doing?" retorted Whisky Jack.

Just then Buster Bear came out of that thicket. For the

first time he saw Peter. "What are you here for?" he growled.

"Nothing," replied Peter so hastily that his tongue almost tripped over itself. "I just happened along."

"Then you better happen to keep on going along," growled Buster, taking a step toward Peter.

Peter hastily ran a short distance. He looked back. Buster wasn't chasing him. He was standing with his head moving from side to side. He seemed to have forgotten Peter already. Was he sleepy? Peter decided to hang around. It is queer how hard it is to do that which we *must* do, however simple it may be, and how easy to do something difficult that we want to do. Buster Bear was killing time as the saying is. He was just fiddling about, knowing that he had to go to bed but putting off doing so just as long as he could. He wasn't hungry. It was of no use to try to make himself think that he was. It wouldn't do to go to bed on a full stomach so Old Mother Nature had taken away his appetite. He may not have known this but it was so. Had he been hungry he would have had an excuse, a good excuse, for not going to bed. And he was sleepy although he wouldn't admit it even to himself. It was bedtime but he didn't want to go to bed, and he didn't intend to go to bed — yet. That is what he told himself anyway.

He had made a good bed. It was a very good bed. He had arranged those boughs so that they made a springy comfortable bed that would keep him off the cold hard ground. It was a good enough bed for anyone. Anyway it was good enough for any Bear.

"I see you have made your bed," said Whisky Jack, who had come down from the Great Mountain just as Buster Bear had.

"Yes," admitted Buster. "Yes, I've made it, but I don't know what I did it for. I don't want to go to sleep. I don't know what possessed me. I saw this thicket and the first thing I knew I was making a bed in the middle of it. Now maybe I won't use it." He yawned.

"That's a queer place to spend the winter," said Whisky Jack, his eye twinkling with mischief.

"Who said I am going to spend the winter there?" grumbled Buster Bear, and tried to stifle another yawn.

"No one said so, but of course you are. You wouldn't have gone to all the trouble of making such a fine bed if you didn't expect to use it for a long time," replied Whisky Jack.

Buster shuffled over to an opening among the trees where he could sit in the sun. He pretended not to have heard what his neighbor had said. He yawned again. He opened his mouth so wide that Whisky Jack could see down his throat.

"I should think you would want to be in or under something to sleep comfortably through the winter, not right out in the open like that with nothing but the sky over you," said Whisky Jack.

"I slept under a windfall last winter. The winter before I slept in a cave. Once I dug a hole under the roots of a big old stump and slept in that. Once more I ask you, who says I am going to sleep out in the open?" growled Buster Bear. Then he shuffled off a short distance and would say nothing more.

Whisky Jack flew off to look for something to eat. Peter Rabbit, who had been hanging around, finally decided that he had learned all he was likely to learn and started down the Crooked Little Path headed for home. Buster Bear wandered around aimlessly but never very far from the thicket where he had made his bed. Late in the afternoon he stood for a long time with his head lifted as he sniffed the wind.

"I think it is going to snow," he muttered. He turned and entered the thicket. He moved a bough here and another there. Then with a sigh he lay down on his bed. He moved this way and that until he was comfortable. He sighed again, closed his eyes, opened them, closed them. He had turned in for the long winter sleep, though probably he didn't know it.

The young hemlock trees growing so close together made a living wall around his bed, a wall that shut out rough Brother North Wind even when he blew his hardest. Only overhead was he unprotected, having only the sky for a roof. Perhaps that is why that very night Old Mother Nature spread over him a soft white blanket and tucked him in snug and warm for the duration — the duration of winter. From time to time she would bring up the snow clouds and make that blanket thicker, and so warmer, while Buster slept and knew nothing at all about it. You are surprised that he should have made his bed under the open sky? Bears do that sometimes.

VI. Each to His Own Way

True progress there could never be
If people didn't disagree.
    — OLD MOTHER NATURE

THAT REDDY FOX is one of the smartest of the Green Forest and Green Meadow folks most folks agree. What many fail to see is that his smartness really is merely good, sound common sense. Reddy is blessed with a lot of that and because of this he seldom makes the mistake of doing anything really foolish.

With more common sense in the world there would be a great deal less trouble in the world.

Reddy was so hungry that he was really starving and becoming desperate. Starvation makes people desperate. For what they do then they should not be judged as are other folks. Just in front of him and back to him sat Bobby Coon. He hadn't seen Reddy. He had just come down from his snug home in a hollow in a big tree where he had slept away the greater part of the winter. He wasn't fully awake yet. The temptation to make a surprise attack from behind was hard for Reddy to resist. Desperation urged him to. Common sense warned him not to. He listened to common sense. Listening to common sense is always a measure of smartness.

Bobby turned his head and saw Reddy crouched behind him in the Crooked Little Path. Instantly he was wide-awake. "Don't do it!" he growled.

Reddy grinned sheepishly. "I don't intend to, Brother Coon. I don't intend to. You are too big and strong for me even if I am desperate," said he.

"What makes you desperate?" asked Bobby.

"Hunger," replied Reddy. "I've never known a harder winter."

"It hasn't been hard for me," said Bobby Coon. "Folks with sense would do as I do — sleep when the weather is cold and food is scarce."

Reddy shook his head. "I don't see how you do it. I can't and it isn't because I haven't sense," said he.

"If I didn't do it how would I get anything to eat?" demanded Bobby.

"The same way I do, by hunting for it. It takes a lot of hunting but most of the time I manage to get something. True I am hungry much of the time, but it is only now and then that I am as badly in need of food as I am now. But I'll find something somewhere. I always have managed to and I guess I always will," replied Reddy.

"I couldn't do it," said Bobby Coon.

"Why couldn't you if I can?" demanded Reddy.

"That is a foolish question," replied Bobby tartly. "Look at me. I'm not built for running about as you are. I'm too heavy, too short in the legs, not the right shape. I'm not built for running and covering long distances any more than you are for climbing trees. There are no Frogs now. There are no fruits. There is no sweet corn. If I couldn't sleep most of the time I would starve. So I sleep, as Mother Nature meant I should."

"Then what are you awake and out for now?" Reddy asked.

"I wake up once in a while and come out to see what the weather is like, usually late in the winter, as I have this time. Then I go back to sleep again for the rest of the winter," explained Bobby.

"Are you hungry now?" demanded Reddy.

37

"Not very. If I should find something tempting I probably would eat it, but it won't matter much whether I do or don't," replied Bobby.

"Imagine that!" sighed Reddy. "And I'm starving, really starving. At that I wouldn't change places with you. Spending all one's time sleeping isn't really living. No, sir, it isn't really living."

"Running about starved or half-starved isn't really living if you ask me. I prefer to sleep," retorted Bobby Coon.

Reddy grinned again. "Each to his own way," said he. "I guess that is the way Mother Nature intends it to be. It is a good thing that folks disagree sometimes. If you had to hunt all winter as I do there would be just so much less food for me."

"I think I'll go back to bed," said Bobby and turned toward his hollow tree.

Reddy watched Bobby climb back up in his hollow tree to go to sleep again for the remainder of the winter.

"I don't know how he does it. I can't do it and I wouldn't if I could. I'm starving, but I would rather starve and know I am alive than to be alive and not know it," muttered Reddy as he trotted on, hoping, as he had been hoping for so long, that somewhere he would find the good meal he so much needed.

Presently ahead of him he heard a familiar sound. It was half whine, half grunt. Someone was talking to himself, complaining. "Prickly Porky wouldn't be happy unless he was complaining about something. Here he is one of the luckiest fellows in all the Great World, for he never really has to go hungry, yet he always is complaining. If there isn't anything to complain about he complains because there isn't. I wonder what he would have to say were he in my place. I doubt if ever in all his life he has been as hungry as I am now," thought Reddy.

Prickly Porky was shuffling along the Crooked Little Path. He had just come down from a tree at one side and was on his way to another. When he saw Reddy the thousand little spears called quills, which were hidden in his coat of long hair, jumped up out of hiding.

"Don't you touch me. Don't you dare try to touch me. You'll be sorry if you do," whined Prickly Porky.

"Are you telling me? Why I wouldn't touch you if I knew you were the last chance in the world for me to get a bite to eat, and goodness knows I need that bite," retorted Reddy.

"I'm glad you've got such good sense," whined Prickly Porky and rattled his thousand little spears most unpleasantly.

"What were you complaining about just now?" asked Reddy.

"Why shouldn't I complain? I'm tired of eating the same kind of food day after day. And there is the bother of having to climb down from a comfortable place to go look for another tree and climb it in order to get a change," whined Prickly Porky.

"You have enough to eat, don't you?" said Reddy.

"Of course I have enough to eat. I have all the Green Forest. Don't ask silly questions," replied Prickly Porky crossly.

"And you never go hungry, really hungry. You never wonder where you are going to get the next meal," said Reddy.

"Of course not. Why should I? I'm not so stupid as all that," retorted Prickly Porky.

"And you don't mind the weather," continued Reddy.

"I don't like bad storms, but who does? I can always go into my den until a storm is over," replied Prickly Porky in his fretful tone of voice.

"And I come along to hear you complaining when you haven't a thing in the world to complain about," said Reddy in disgust.

"I have too. I told you I'm tired of the same kind of bark and buds day after day, and it is such a bother to have to keep changing trees," whined Prickly Porky.

"If it were not for those little spears you carry about you would never again have to bother to change trees. I've just one wish for you," said Reddy.

"What is that?" asked Prickly Porky.

"That you may know what it is to be as hungry as I am and not know where to look for something to eat. Then you'll have something to complain about," retorted Reddy sharply and trotted off.

"But I like to complain," whined Prickly Porky. What a lot of Prickly Porkys there are in the world!

VII. Plenty and Nothing

A thing is good or it is bad,
Makes you happy, makes you sad,
According to your point of view;
The answer really lies in you.

— OLD MOTHER NATURE

REDDY FOX WAS at the winter yard of Lightfoot the Deer
to one side of the Crooked Little Path. He had come to pay
a call. It was a yard without a fence, but it had a wall around it,
a wall of snow. It was a place where the Deer kept the snow
trampled down in paths that crossed and recrossed among the
trees and brush. On the tender twigs and buds of these the Deer
would depend for food. They had begun making that yard with

the coming of the first snow. At first it had been much smaller. As they browsed on the boughs within easy reach they kept making those paths longer and thus made the yard bigger.

But there came a time when the snow was so deep they seldom went outside the paths already made. Icy crust formed and if they tried to leave the paths their sharp hoofs broke through, and the hard crust cut their slim legs. More snow fell so that outside the yard it was up to their shoulders. They couldn't plunge through it. They gave up trying. They were prisoners in their own yard.

At first they didn't mind. They were very comfortable. After all there was nowhere that they wanted to go. When they were lying down the walls of snow shut away cold wind. There was plenty to eat. But there came a time when there wasn't plenty to eat. They had stripped the boughs within easy reach. They had to stretch for higher boughs. Even then they could not get enough to keep them from being always hungry. They became thin at the very time when they needed to be fat to withstand the cold weather. And as they became thinner they began to lose strength.

Lightfoot was the first to see Reddy Fox. "We have a caller," said he.

Mrs. Lightfoot lifted her head anxiously to look. When she saw Reddy she gave a low sigh of thankfulness that it wasn't Old Man Coyote, or Yowler the Bobcat, or Puma the Mountain Lion, especially the latter. When the fawns were very small she

43

might have feared Reddy. Now they were too big for him. That is they were unless they should become too weak from lack of food.

"It is a long time since I last saw you folks. I hope I find you well," said Reddy.

"As well as can be expected considering the hard times," replied Lightfoot.

"What do you know about hard times? Some folks seem never to know when they are well off. Here you are with food all around you and you talk of hard times. It is we who must hunt for and catch our food, and at times like this can't find it, who know what hard times are. I tell you, Neighbor Lightfoot, Mrs. Reddy and I have been on the edge of starvation this winter," said Reddy.

"That is where we Deer are right now," replied Lightfoot quietly.

Reddy stared. "Is that a joke?" he asked.

Lightfoot raised himself on his hind feet and stretched as high as he could trying to reach a few twigs above him. He failed. Had he been up on top of the snow as Reddy was he could have reached them easily. But he was too heavy and his hoofs were too sharp for the crust on the snow. He couldn't even get up on it.

"You see; plenty and nothing," said he.

"No, I don't see. What do you mean by plenty and nothing?" retorted Reddy.

"Plenty of food in sight and nothing to eat," replied Light-

foot. "We can look up and see plenty of food beyond our reach. We can look outside our yard and see plenty, but it also is beyond our reach. And we have eaten all save a twig here and there that we can reach. Do you still wonder what we know about hard times?"

"I beg your pardon," said Reddy Fox.

"For what?" asked Lightfoot the Deer.

"For thinking that you had no real cause for complaining about hard times. I've learned something," replied Reddy.

"What have you learned?" Lightfoot wanted to know.

"I've learned how mistaken one can be about his neighbors when he thinks he knows all about them. I thought we who eat meat were the only ones who were in danger of starving because of deep snow and ice storms and bitter cold. I know there is plenty of the kind of food you Deer eat, so I couldn't see any reason why you should go hungry. I never thought of you being prisoners in your own yard with not enough food to last," said Reddy. "Aren't those youngsters getting weak?" he asked as if it were an afterthought.

Lightfoot looked at him sharply and lifted a forefoot to paw away a little snow. Reddy grinned. He knew that Lightfoot meant him to see how hard and sharp-edged that hoof was. "I'm not that hungry," said he.

"It is just as well," replied Lightfoot. "Mrs. Lightfoot and I are still strong."

Reddy pretended to take no notice of this. "Hello! See who is here!" he exclaimed.

A round brown head had appeared over the edge of the snow. It was Little Joe Otter. Little Joe Otter isn't little, not now. Of course he was little once and that is when he got the name of Little Joe and he has been called by it ever since. He is much heavier than Reddy Fox which of course means that he is bigger. But his legs are so short that he doesn't stand as high as Reddy.

"Hi! Isn't this grand weather!" cried Little Joe.

Reddy Fox said nothing. Lightfoot and Mrs. Lightfoot and the two young Deer said nothing. Little Joe didn't notice. "It is the best winter I've known for a long time," he continued.

"I'm glad someone likes it," said Reddy.

Little Joe looked at him with a funny expression of surprise on his face. "Don't you?" he demanded.

"No, I don't," said Reddy in a most decided tone.

"Nor I," said Lightfoot.

"Nor I," said Mrs. Lightfoot. The two young Deer said nothing but it was plain that they felt the same way.

"Why don't you like it?" demanded Little Joe.

"Would you like it if you were starving because of it?" asked Lightfoot.

"No. But why starve? If I couldn't find food in one place I would try another. I would go where it is. That is what I do. Anyone with common sense would do that," said Little Joe.

"What if you couldn't go where it is? What would you do

48

then? I'll tell you what you would do — you would starve," retorted Lightfoot.

"They are prisoners in their own yard because the snow is so deep," explained Reddy.

"Oh!" exclaimed Little Joe.

"Too much snow and too much icy crust," said Reddy Fox. "It makes it too hard for an honest Fox to get an honest living. Mice are mostly safe under the snow. Jumper the Hare with his snowshoes can get around faster and better than I can. Peter Rabbit is just as safe in his bramble-tangles as at any other time. Thunderer the Grouse and Mrs. Grouse can see me too far away for me to have a chance of catching one of them. Almost every minute I am awake I have to spend hunting and am nearly starved most of the time and hungry all the time. If I could have plenty to eat I wouldn't mind the cold and snow."

All the Deer nodded. "If we could get around we wouldn't mind either. Winters when there is little snow we get along nicely. We can always go where there is food. We can't now because there is too much snow," said Lightfoot.

"I love it!" declared Little Joe. "It is great fun to slide when there is a crust. Watch me!"

The Deer yard was at the foot of a low hill. Little Joe made his way to the top of this. There was about an inch of light snow covering a hard smooth crust. At the top of the hill Little Joe turned, ran a few steps and threw himself flat on his stomach with his hind legs straight out behind and his forelegs back and

49

close to his sides. Down he slid for a little way, making a fur-row in the soft snow. When he stopped he ran again and once more slid.

"That is what I call fun," cried Little Joe as he rejoined the others. "Traveling is fun when you can do a lot of sliding like that. Why don't you try it?"

Reddy grinned. Then he chuckled. "What are you laughing at?" demanded Little Joe Otter good-naturedly.

"What would Lightfoot do with his legs?" chuckled Reddy. "For that matter what would I do with mine? They are not made for stretching back the way yours are. Sliding may be fun for you, and so you may like snow and ice as you say you do, but it is hard on some of the rest of us."

"I'll say it is!" said Lightfoot.

"I suppose you will be telling us next that you like the fun of sliding so much that you don't mind going hungry," said Reddy.

"But I don't go hungry. Do I look as if I do?" retorted Little Joe.

The others had to admit that he didn't look as if he had been going hungry. They agreed that they never had seen him look-ing in better condition. "It is just a matter of eating food that you can get no matter what the weather," said Little Joe as if he thought that that was the simplest matter in the world.

"Meaning what?" asked Lightfoot.

"Fish," replied Little Joe promptly. "There are always fish for the catching no matter what the weather."

"I wish I had one now," sighed Reddy. "Two or three wouldn't be too many. Where do you find these fish that are always to be caught no matter what the weather? I've never been lucky enough to find any."

"That's because you don't go where they are," said Little Joe. Then he looked a wee bit foolish. "You have to swim," he added.

"And you have to have a waterproof coat and dive and hold your breath and — and fish are for those who can catch them. We can't. I still say this is an awful winter," said Reddy.

"I love it," retorted Little Joe.

VIII. Fun and Fishing

In every day a little fun
Should be enjoyed by everyone.
— LITTLE JOE OTTER

LITTLE JOE OTTER and all his family thoroughly believe in that saying of his and they live accordingly. Summer or winter they somehow find time for a little play. In summer they delight to play in water. In winter they seem to get just as much fun playing in snow. They play together and they play by themselves. Play is fun. Of course.

"Plenty of fun and fish make a good disposition," says Little Joe and seems to prove it. Anyway he has the fun, he has the fish, and he has the good disposition.

"What brings you way over here in the Green Forest?" asked Lightfoot the Deer.

"Fun," replied Little Joe.

Lightfoot shook his head sadly. "There is no fun here in the Green Forest," said he.

"Come with me and I'll show you fun," said Little Joe.

Lightfoot shook his head. Mrs. Lightfoot shook her head. The two young Deer shook their heads. In their big soft eyes were sadness and fear and despair. "We can't even go looking for food because of the snow. We can move about only where we have kept it trodden down, and we have eaten nearly all the food we can reach. How can there be fun where there is hunger? There is no fun in the Green Forest," said Lightfoot.

"If you can find fun in the Green Forest you are lucky. I can get around, but like Lightfoot and his family I am hungry and I find no fun in the Green Forest or anywhere else for that matter," said Reddy Fox.

Little Joe spoke softly. "I'm sorry," said he. "I didn't understand."

"I guess if neighbors really understood all about each other they would all be happier," said Reddy. "But there is no fun in being hungry when there is nothing to eat. I can tell you that, Neighbor Otter. Just where do you expect to have fun? What kind of fun?"

53

"There's a certain place up Laughing Brook which is almost always unfrozen and where the water is deep enough and the bank high enough for a slippery slide. I am going there to make one," said Little Joe.

"Do you mean you will slide down into the water?" asked Lightfoot.

"Of course," replied Little Joe.

All the Deer shivered. Reddy shivered. "And he calls that fun. How queer some folks are," said he.

"Come along and try it," invited Little Joe. "You might feel differently," he added.

"I'm sure I would — wet and cold," grinned Reddy.

So Little Joe went running and sliding on his way. The others watched him out of sight and somehow they felt better for Little Joe's visit. Reddy started for home, then changed his mind. He would follow Little Joe and see if he really would make a slippery slide down into the cold water. He shivered again at the thought.

Little Joe's trail was easy to follow, very easy. There were not only his footprints but a furrow in the light top snow made by his dragging tail, and at times a bigger furrow where he had found a place to slide a few feet.

Reddy approached Laughing Brook cautiously. Long ago he learned that caution is wisdom. He left the trail and circled around to a place where without being seen he could see the black cold water where Laughing Brook was not frozen. The opposite bank was steep. Little Joe Otter was at the top of it looking down at the water. Suddenly he threw himself down the bank headfirst, his legs straight behind him and his arms at his sides. Down he slid plop into the black cold water. Reddy shivered. He waited and waited for Little Joe to come up. It seemed a long time before he did. When he did he had a fish in his mouth.

Reddy began to drool. Yes, sir, he began to drool. His mouth watered so that drops fell from the corners. He ran his tongue out and licked his lips. He quivered all over. To quiver is to shake with longing, desire. What made him quiver? That fish. Yes, sir, Reddy was quivering because of that fish.

Little Joe climbed out on the ice with it and put it down at his feet. He sat looking at it as if uncertain whether to eat it at once or leave it until later. It was clear that he wasn't very hungry. Reddy was. It was because he was so hungry that he was drooling as he kept his eyes fixed on that fish. He was so hungry that it seemed to him that he must run out and grab that fish. He didn't. No, sir, he didn't try anything as foolish as that. Little Joe Otter was too big and too strong and too good a fighter to be robbed that way by any Fox, even one quite desperate with hunger. So Reddy remained hidden, watching and quivering and drooling.

Little Joe climbed the bank where it was low, went to the top where it was highest and slid down headfirst just where Reddy had seen him slide down before. He was making a slippery slide. He was sliding for fun just as a boy slides on a sled or older folks on a toboggan. Plop into the water he went. Would he come up with another fish? Reddy watched eagerly. The happy slider wasn't out of sight so long this time. His round head bobbed up almost at once. He had nothing in his mouth.

He climbed out just where he had before, took a bite out of the fish lying there, and went on up to the top of the slippery slide. Again he slid down plop into the water and again he climbed out almost at once. This time he hardly glanced at that fish, but hurried up the bank for another slide. Each time he went down a little faster. That slippery slide was growing smoother with use, more slippery. Each time Little Joe disappeared in the water Reddy seemed to feel a chill. You see Reddy doesn't possess such a sleek waterproof coat over a thick fur coat, so it was hard to understand how anyone could swim and dive in such cold water and still be warm and comfortable.

This time Little Joe was gone so long that Reddy began to wonder what had become of him. "Perhaps he isn't coming back. Perhaps he has gone somewhere under the ice. Perhaps he has a hole in the bank with an entrance under water such as Jerry Muskrat has. If he doesn't come back I'll have that fish. I hope he doesn't come back," thought he.

Just then Little Joe popped his head out of water and he had another fish. It was bigger than the first one. He climbed out

and laid it beside the other. Reddy drooled more than ever. He quivered more than ever. Little Joe sat beside the two fish looking at them. This time he didn't take even a bite.

"I wonder how it would feel to be so full of good food I couldn't eat more. And I wonder what he will do with those fish. I know what I would do with them if I had them," thought Reddy and grinned ruefully.

The next time Little Joe plopped into the water Reddy moved quickly. By the time that round head appeared again Reddy was flat behind a shelter much nearer those fish. Again he changed his position when Little Joe was out of sight. This time Little Joe stopped beside the fish. Was he going to eat them? Was he going to take them away? Reddy had harder work than ever to keep from rushing out and trying to take one of them. He didn't. He kept still, all but the quivering. That was self-control. Self-control is one of the most important things in the world. It is one of the first things little furred and feathered folk learn or they do not live long. Perhaps Little Joe didn't want those fish. Anyway perhaps he might leave one. Reddy watched and quivered and drooled.

He kept his eyes fixed on Little Joe at the top of his slippery slide. He just sat there for the longest time. It seemed as if he never would go down. But he did and the very instant he touched the water Reddy dashed over to those fish, grabbed one, and by the time Little Joe's head popped above water was out of sight behind some brush. There he ate that fish. It was big as fish go in Laughing Brook, big enough for a good meal.

As he lay there licking his lips a wonderful change took place. Everything seemed different. Nothing looked the same. He suddenly liked the snow and ice that only so short a time before had seemed dreadful. It was good to be alive and over in the Green Forest. The Great World was a wonderful place filled with hope and the promise of good things for those smart enough to get them. Little Joe Otter was right in saying that there was fun in the Green Forest for those who looked for it. It was fun just to lie there with a full stomach and plan how he would get that other fish. It would be more fun to get the fish and still more fun to take it home to Mrs. Reddy and watch her grin when she saw it. That fish in his stomach made all the difference in the world.

If Little Joe missed that fish he made no sign. He didn't appear to notice when the second one disappeared. You see he wasn't hungry. He just didn't give a thought to those fish but only to the fun he was having on his slippery slide. If later he should miss those fish he wouldn't care. There were more where those had come from and catching some would be fun.

IX. The Magic of Sister South Wind

Just a light caress may give
Hope and faith and will to live.
— OLD MOTHER NATURE

LIGHTFOOT THE DEER remembered no winter as hard
as this had been. Snow had fallen early and often and now for
a long time had lain deep in the Green Forest and on the
Green Meadows, so deep that only those light enough, or with
wide-spreading toes with hair between, like Jumper the Hare,
or with little spreading points like Thunderer the Grouse,

60

could walk on it. Lightfoot, Mrs. Lightfoot and their twins couldn't. So they were prisoners in the yard they had trodden out for themselves in the Green Forest. Now they were really starving. Lightfoot and Mrs. Lightfoot were as near despair as ever they had been.

Then one afternoon Lightfoot felt a light touch on his nose. It was so light that he wasn't quite sure he had felt it. He lifted his head and held his nose high. At first he felt nothing and was disappointed. Then came that ever-so-light touch again, a soft caress. There was no doubt about it this time. His big soft eyes, which had been dull with suffering and despair, grew bright with hope. Mrs. Lightfoot saw it.

"What is it?" she asked.

"Gentle Sister South Wind has come!" cried Lightfoot. "No one can help us as she can if she will, and I am sure she will."

"I will," whispered gentle Sister South Wind in one of Lightfoot's big ears. "Of course I will. That is what I have come for. I will set you free. When I am through you will no longer be prisoners but free to go where you will, where the food is."

Mrs. Lightfoot heard her. The twins heard her and for the first time in many days there was cheerfulness in that yard.

"What can she do?" asked one of the twins doubtfully, for this was their first winter and they knew nothing about gentle Sister South Wind.

"She is too gentle to do much," said the other.

"Be patient, my dears, and you will see," replied their

61

mother. "She can set us free more quickly than even jolly, bright Mr. Sun can without her help. She can take away this snow even faster than rain could. If only she will stay we will soon be able to leave here and get the food we so much need."

"I'll stay," whispered Sister South Wind in the listening ears of the four Deer. "I have been hurrying to get here, for down in the land of warmth I heard that Old Man Winter had been hard and cruel to you and others living here, and your need of me is very great."

"But what can you do against Old Man Winter?" asked one of the young Deer and added, "You are too soft and gentle."

Sister South Wind blew softly in his ears and kissed his nose and her breath was warm and sweet. "I can make the snow disappear and the ice turn to water and the warmth I have brought from the land of warmth will drive Old Man Winter back and back to the Far North whence he came. Despite his roughness and his toughness and his harshness he will become helpless before me. Watch, my children, and you shall see what gentle persistence can do," she said.

"It is even so," said Lightfoot, who had been listening. "Gentle Sister South Wind is the friend of all, and all through the Green Forest and over the Green Meadows wherever she goes there is rejoicing. Today we are hungry, but — "

"I'll say we are," interrupted one of the young Deer.

"But tomorrow we shall eat, or the day after anyway. Is it not so, Sister South Wind?" continued Lightfoot.

"It is even so. I have come," replied Sister South Wind softly.

The voice of rough Brother North Wind is a roar, sometimes a shriek. The voice of gentle Sister South Wind is a whisper that becomes a low murmur like the soft crooning of a lullaby. Through the long night Lightfoot the Deer listened to it and the gnawing emptiness within him was easier to bear for the voice of gentle Sister South Wind was sweet with the promise of freedom to move about. Freedom to move about meant a full stomach, and a full stomach meant a return of strength and the joy of living. So Lightfoot listened and for the first time in many days and nights was free of a great fear, the fear of starvation.

In the morning jolly, round, bright Mr. Sun, looking down from the blue, blue sky on the yard of the Deer in the Green Forest, saw Lightfoot standing with his head held high and his ears spread wide. Beside him was Mrs. Lightfoot, her head across his shoulders and her ears spread wide. Just back of them were the two young Deer, the twins, their ears spread wide. Mr. Sun smiled more brightly than ever for he knew why those ears were so widely spread. He knew that they were listening to the magic of gentle Sister South Wind.

"Listen!" said Lightfoot.

Mrs. Lightfoot and the twins listened even more closely than they had been listening. "What is it?" asked one. "I hear nothing but the murmur of Sister South Wind."

"There!" exclaimed Lightfoot.

63

All heard it then, faintly at first but growing clearer as they listened. "It is the sound of running water and it comes from all around us. Next to Sister South Wind's voice it is the sweetest sound I have heard for a long, long time," said Lightfoot and drew a long breath that ended in a deep sigh of happiness.

The twins looked this way and that way. "I don't see any running water," said one.

"It is under the snow," replied their father.

"What makes it run and why haven't we heard it running before?" asked the young Deer.

"It is the magic of gentle Sister South Wind that makes it run, and you haven't heard it before because she hasn't been here. She is turning the snow to water and the water is running to Laughing Brook and soon we shall be free," replied his mother.

"I hear the fir trees and the pine trees and the hemlock trees whispering. All winter they have moaned and there has been distress and sadness in the sound of it, but now they are whispering and there is happiness in it as in the sound of running water. They know that Sister South Wind is here and what her coming means. All the trees know. It is part of her magic," said Lightfoot. Then he tried wading in the snow. There was no longer a crust and the snow was not as deep as it had been but it was still too deep for him to get far.

However he did break a way through to some brush and young trees they had not been able to reach before and at once they began happily browsing on the young twigs with their tender buds.

Lightfoot bit off a twig from a young maple. It was the sweetest taste he had had for months. A clear drop of what looked like water formed at the place where the twig had been bitten off and hung there glistening. Lightfoot saw it and licked it off. It was sap, not water. Sap was being drawn up from the roots where it had been stored all through the long winter. What had started it? The magic of gentle Sister South Wind.

That night the snow settled enough for Lightfoot and his family to leave their yard for good. Wherever they went there was rejoicing, for everybody knew that gentle Sister South Wind was making the Green Forest and the Green Meadows ready for the coming of sweet Mistress Spring, and that she wasn't far behind.

X. Peter's Blindness

The truly blind we may excuse;
Not those with eyes they do not use.
— OLD MOTHER NATURE

THAT DOESN'T SOUND reasonable, but it is true. It is astonishing how little some really bright eyes see. Are your eyes like that?

Peter Rabbit was tired of cold weather. There were many others with the same feeling. Gentle Sister South Wind had come but the ground was still covered with snow. The Smiling Pool and the Big River were still covered with ice. Rough

Brother North Wind still blew cold, and Jack Frost pinched hard at night. Peter was very, very tired of it all.

"Dee, dee, dee! Chickadee, dee, dee!" cried Tommy Tit, clinging upside down to a twig to drink a drop of water from the tip of a small icicle that had begun to melt.

"What are you so cheerful about?" demanded Peter.

"Winter will soon be gone!" cried Tommy Tit.

"Who says so?" snapped Peter rather crossly.

"I do! Dee, dee, dee, I do!" cried Tommy Tit cheerily.

"What do you know about it?" demanded Peter.

"I can see the signs," replied Tommy Tit.

"What signs?" Peter wanted to know.

"The signs that Old Man Winter soon will be gone, and sweet Mistress Spring is on her way," explained Tommy Tit.

"Pooh!" exclaimed Peter. "There aren't any such signs. I've been watching for them and there isn't one anywhere."

"Dee, dee, dee, dee! What is the matter with your eyes, Peter Rabbit?" cried Tommy Tit.

"Nothing," replied Peter indignantly. "Not a thing. They are just as good as yours." This wasn't quite true, but undoubtedly Peter thought it was. There are few among the folks in fur with eyes as good as those of the feathered folk.

"Then why don't you use them?" demanded Tommy Tit, swinging head down from the tip of a twig.

"I do. Who says I don't?" retorted Peter crossly.

"But I have seen spring signs and you haven't!" cried Tommy

67

Tit. "If your eyes are as good as mine, and you had used them, you would have seen those signs too."

"I don't believe you have seen a single sign that Old Man Winter is nearly through and Mistress Spring is on her way," declared Peter flatly.

"It is funny how some folks can see and still be blind," said Tommy Tit.

"Meaning me?" asked Peter sharply.

"I mentioned no names," retorted Tommy Tit. "But if I was sitting right under a sign and couldn't see it I would call that a sort of blindness."

Peter was sitting beneath a young maple tree. He looked up through the branches. They were as bare as they had been all winter. He looked sharply at Tommy Tit. Tommy appeared to be very busy, not noticing Peter at all. Peter looked back up in the tree. He saw nothing that looked to him like a sign.

"There is no sign up there," he declared flatly.

"Now I know you are blind. You have eyes but you can't see. Anyway you don't see," said Tommy Tit.

At that Peter quite lost his temper. He stamped angrily. "Show me a sign. Just show me," he commanded.

"Dee, dee, dee!" cried Tommy Tit merrily. "Why should I show you what you should see for yourself? That is," he added, "if you really have good eyes."

Peter did his best to glare up at Tommy Tit, but he wasn't very successful. He hasn't the glaring kind of eyes. They must be fierce to glare. Peter's are timid and gentle. "You won't show because you can't. There is nothing to show. I can see all over that tree and there isn't a thing in it. It is bare. It is just as bare as it was the day the last leaf fell," declared Peter.

Tommy Tit's bright little eyes twinkled and snapped. The angrier Peter became the more those little eyes twinkled and snapped. He was teasing Peter and enjoying it. Queer how some nice folks like to tease others.

"It is bare and it isn't," replied Tommy Tit.

"That isn't sense. If it is bare it is bare, and if it isn't bare it isn't bare. It can't be both," retorted Peter.

"Then let's put it this way: it looks bare, but isn't," replied Tommy Tit.

"But it is!" exclaimed Peter, and stamped again.

"What are those little red things on every little twig?" asked Tommy Tit.

"Buds," replied Peter promptly. "Leaf buds. But they don't count. They were there from the time the leaves fell last fall."

"But they do count!" cried Tommy Tit. "My goodness, I should say they do! Dee, dee, dee, I should say they do!"

"How?" demanded Peter crossly.

"If they were not there there would be no leaves next summer, and a tree without leaves can't live. And you say they don't count!" cried Tommy Tit.

"Well," admitted Peter, "of course they count in one way." He stopped to scratch a long ear with a long hind foot. "But,"

69

he added, "they don't count in the way I mean and you know it."

"Have you really looked at those buds?" asked Tommy Tit.

"Of course I have. I'm looking at them now. What about them?" said Peter.

"Don't be stupid! Dee, dee, dee, don't be stupid!" cried Tommy Tit.

"I'm not stupid!" snapped Peter.

"Then don't tell me that those little red buds look just the same as they have all winter long," protested Tommy Tit.

Peter stared up on the tree. "Just the same," he began, then paused.

"Well?" said Tommy Tit.

"Maybe they are bigger than they were," admitted Peter.

"There is no maybe about it and you know it. They are twice as big as they were, and if your eyes are as good as mine you would see that they swell a little bigger each day. And that's the sign I said was up in this tree. If Old Man Winter wasn't going pretty quick those buds wouldn't have begun to swell."

"Oh," said Peter lamely. Then he added, "Are there any more signs?"

"Have you been over to the Green Forest within the last few days?" asked Tommy Tit.

"What has that to do with it?" demanded Peter.

"I saw some spring signs over there this morning," replied Tommy Tit.

"I'm going over there," declared Peter.

"Dee, dee, dee! You wouldn't see them if you found them. Dee, dee, dee!" cried Tommy Tit.

"I would too!" cried Peter indignantly.

Tommy Tit merely chuckled his happy throaty little chuckle. "Good luck to you. I've got business over in the Old Orchard." Away he flitted before Peter could ask more about those spring signs.

Of course Peter just *had* to go over to the Green Forest. Curiosity would give him no peace. Besides, he wanted to believe that he could see anything that Tommy Tit could see. He didn't want to believe that those tiny black eyes saw more than his own did. So the first chance he got he ran over to the Green Forest. There he wandered about aimlessly. Finally he saw Happy Jack Squirrel.

"What are you doing over here?" asked Happy Jack.

"Just looking around," replied Peter. "I'm tired of winter, aren't you?"

"Well, I won't say that I am sorry that Mistress Spring is on the way," replied Happy Jack.

"How do you know she is?" demanded Peter.

"Signs," replied Happy Jack. "Spring signs."

"Have you really seen any?" asked Peter eagerly.

"Of course," replied Happy Jack. "Anyone who gets about and keeps his eyes open must have seen them."

"I get about and I keep my eyes open, but I haven't seen any signs of spring," said Peter. Then he remembered the swollen buds on the maple tree. "That is, I haven't seen anything that I believe is a sign," he corrected himself, and added, "I don't believe in signs anyway."

Just then a drop of something fell at Peter's feet. "There's one," said Happy Jack, who was right over Peter in a maple tree.

XI. Peter Finds His Eyes

In little signs, can you but read them,
Are promises when most you need them.

— OLD MOTHER NATURE

A DROP OF SOMETHING had fallen at Peter's feet.

"There's one," said Happy Jack.

"One what?" asked Peter, looking puzzled.

"Didn't you just say that you don't believe in signs?" asked Happy Jack.

Peter nodded. "I did. What of it?" said he.

"That drop was a sign, and here's another," replied Happy Jack. A second drop fell.

"Signs of what?" demanded Peter crossly.

"Signs of spring," said Happy Jack.

Peter blinked. "I don't believe it. What have drops of water to do with spring?" retorted Peter.

"Those were not drops of water; they were drops of sap," said Happy Jack. He stopped to lick a drop from where he had bitten off a twig.

"Is it good?" asked Peter.

"Of course it is good. If it were not do you think I would bother to cut off twigs to get it?" retorted Happy Jack.

"Where does it come from?" asked Peter innocently.

Happy Jack looked down at Peter Rabbit in disgust. "Didn't you see where it came from?" he demanded. He bit off another twig. Peter saw a drop glisten in the sunlight as it fell.

"I know it drips out of the tree where you bit off that twig, but where did it come from before that? And how do you know it is a sign that Mistress Spring will soon be here?" said Peter.

"How should I know where it comes from? I suppose it comes from the roots deep down in the ground. What I do know is that it is a sign. Yes, sir, it is a sign that Mistress Spring isn't far away. That I *know*," replied Happy Jack.

Peter Rabbit is nothing if not persistent. "How do you know that?" he demanded.

Happy Jack licked off another drop of sap. He looked down at Peter pityingly. "I know because I know," said he, which really was no answer at all. "I've known it ever since I was a year old," he continued. "Sap is good. It is sweet. This kind is, anyway. I like it. I guess it is good for me. But the only time when it is at its best, and when I can get all I want, is when Old Man Winter is getting ready to leave and Mistress Spring is getting near. It has been just so ever since I can remember. So when there has been no sap since the first cold weather and then one day I happen to bite a twig and the sap begins to drip, I know that sweet Mistress Spring is near. If that isn't a sign, what is it?"

Peter scratched a long ear with a long hind foot. "I guess it must be," said he.

"I don't guess; I know," declared Happy Jack. "And I'm not the only one who knows it," he added. "Downy the Wood-pecker and his Cousin Sapsucker like to drink sap, and both know that they can get it at its best, which is now, only when Mistress Spring is almost here. They know and I know. But if you want another sign go look in Laughing Brook," said Happy Jack.

At first Peter had no intention of doing anything of the kind. In the first place he disliked to believe that Happy Jack knew anything unknown to himself. Going over to the Laughing Brook would be admitting that very thing. A lot of people are like Peter.

But curiosity was too much for him. He hopped away in another direction, but when he was out of Happy Jack's sight he circled around to Laughing Brook. He came to it where the water was deepest and running under ice that reached from bank to bank. It had been that way ever since it first froze over in early winter.

"I knew it," muttered Peter. "There is no sign here. That fellow sent me over here for a joke." His wobbly little nose twitched with indignation and he chewed on nothing at all, a habit of his. He stared up Laughing Brook and down Laughing Brook but saw only snow and ice. He heard the gurgle of the running water under the ice.

"Looking for something?" asked a harsh voice. Blacky the Crow dropped down on an old stump on the opposite bank.

"No," replied Peter shortly. "There is nothing to look for."

"I thought you might be looking for a spring sign in Laughing Brook," said Blacky, his sharp eyes twinkling.

"Why should I look in Laughing Brook for a sign of spring? Tell me that," retorted Peter.

"No reason. Caw, caw, caw! No reason at all if you are not interested," replied Blacky.

"I don't believe in signs," said Peter.

"Too bad," replied Blacky. "You miss a lot if you can't read signs when you see them."

"Who says I can't read signs? I said I don't believe in them," retorted Peter.

"If you could see and read them you would believe in them,"

said Blacky. "There are some things I like to know are going to happen before they do happen. It helps a lot sometimes. For instance, I feel a lot better for knowing that Mistress Spring is almost here."

"How do you know that?" demanded Peter.

"Signs, Peter! Signs! I saw some in Laughing Brook this very morning, and I feel a lot better for it. Caw, caw, caw!" With this Blacky flew away.

"Wait a minute!" cried Peter. "Tell me what those signs are!" But all he got from Blacky was a derisive "Caw, caw, caw!"

Once more Peter stared at Laughing Brook and now it seemed to him that sound from under the ice really was laughter. Was Laughing Brook laughing at him? Of course it was only the sound of running water, but he couldn't get rid of that feeling of being laughed at.

He went on down one bank. There were places where the water ran too swiftly to freeze. It looked black and cold. Peter shivered. It didn't look in the least springlike. At last he came to a little swamp just above the Smiling Pool. It spread out there and was very shallow. Peter found it hard to get about without getting his feet wet. Suddenly almost at his very feet he saw the sign. He saw it without seeing it. That is, he didn't recognize it as a sign.

Peter was staring at something in a little open spot that was wet but where some snow had not yet melted. There at the very edge of the snow were two odd little plants with their feet in the water as it were. One seeing them for the first time might well be excused for failing to recognize them at once as plants. There were no leaves, no stems, just two reddish-brown and greenish things not unlike certain sea shells with a narrow opening on one side that you may have seen. Or they might have reminded you of curving pointed hoods such as you have seen in pictures of the monks of old.

For perhaps two full minutes Peter stared at them. He knew what they were. Of course. He had seen such plants about this time of year ever since he could remember, and each year when he saw them for the first time it was with this same feeling of surprise so great that it was difficult really to believe his own eyes.

Presently he leaned towards them and wiggled his wobbly little nose while he sniffed. At once his nose told him that his eyes were not fooling him. There was a smell that instantly reminded him of Jimmy Skunk. It was very like the perfume that Jimmy carries, but not strong and unpleasant like that.

Suddenly he kicked up his heels in the funny way he sometimes does when he is excited or in high spirits, feeling extra good. "Skunk cabbage!" cried Peter, and again kicked up his long heels.

"Caw, caw, caw! What are you so pleased about?" called Blacky the Crow circling overhead.

"Skunk cabbage!" cried Peter, and kicked up his heels again.

"What of it? Didn't you ever see skunk cabbage before?" asked Blacky.

"Of course I have," replied Peter indignantly. "I've seen it ever since I can remember. It is the first plant to come up and to flower. It is — " Peter paused and a funny look came over his face.

"Well, what is it?" prompted Blacky.

"Why," said Peter, looking as if he felt a bit foolish, "when the skunk cabbage comes up winter is about over. It is — " He paused again.

"Go on," said Blacky. "Say it."

"It is a sign that Mistress Spring isn't far away," admitted Peter.

"I thought you didn't believe in signs," said Blacky.

"I believe in these," replied Peter, looking down at the two odd little plants. "I have to even if there are snow and ice almost everywhere. I don't doubt any more. There are some signs that a fellow has to believe." He looked down at the queer little reddish-brown and greenish hoods. "I wonder," said he.

"What do you wonder?" asked Blacky.

"I wonder how they know it is time to grow. I wonder what makes the sap start up the maple trees when snow and ice still cover the ground," said Peter.

"I guess you'll have to keep on wondering unless you ask Old Mother Nature," replied Blacky. "It is enough for me to know that they are sure signs of better times that will soon be here. Caw, caw, caw, that's enough for me." He turned and disappeared over the tops of the trees.

XII. Yowler Makes a Mistake

Lives one so wise as ne'er to make
An error or a bad mistake?
— YOWLER THE BOBCAT

YOWLER HAS MADE many mistakes in his time and will admit it. Usually he has profited by them. They have taught him lessons which he will never forget. So you see mistakes are not without use to the very ones who make them. One of the mistakes Yowler made cost him some aches and pains and a lot of disappointment. He should have known better than to make such a mistake. He does know better now and isn't likely ever to repeat it.

The first people to set up housekeeping in the Green Forest each year are Mr. and Mrs. Hooty the Great Horned Owls. Stout and hardy folk are Mr. and Mrs. Hooty and they do not wait for the coming of sweet Mistress Spring. By the time she does arrive Hooty's children are half-grown. It is in midwinter that Hooty and Mrs. Hooty decide where they are going to have their home and set about preparing it for the season.

They are opportunists. That means that they believe in making the most of any opportunity they come across. So they rarely go to the trouble of building a whole new nest. According to their ideas that would be sheer waste of time and labor when they know just where there is a home ready, or almost ready, to move right into. So they look over last year's nests of Redtail the Hawk or of some other member of the Hawk family, and of Blacky the Crow. Having decided which one will require the least fixing to put it in condition for their needs, they take possession.

None of the other feathered folk has even thought of nesting when Mrs. Hooty begins sitting on two big eggs and keeping them warm, when rough Brother North Wind is howling through the Green Forest and drifting snow over everything and everybody. Before others even know where they are going to make their homes Hooty and Mrs. Hooty are pridefully

watching two down-clad youngsters grow bigger every day, and are hunting far and wide for food to satisfy those growing appetites.

This year they had taken a nest which had been used each

year for several years by Redtail the Hawk. Mr. and Mrs. Redtail were planning to use it again this season. Hooty didn't know this, but it would have made no difference if he had known it. They would have to build somewhere else, that was all. This nest was in a tall tree near the Crooked Little Path. It was a good nest and little had to be done to it. Now with the first signs of coming spring it contained two sturdy babies who looked quite as fierce as their parents and whose appetites were tremendous.

A number of the forest folk knew of these young Owls, but that part of the Green Forest was considered a good place to stay away from. You see most folks have wholesome respect for the great cruel claws and stout hooked bills of those Owls. It just happened that Yowler the Bobcat was one of those who didn't know of that nest until quite by accident he chanced that way and discovered it.

What first drew his attention to it was the finding of a Mouse on the ground at the foot of a tree. That Mouse had been freshly killed. Yowler, being very hungry, just bolted it down and then began to look about in the hope of finding more bounty. High up in the tree he could see the black mass of sticks of which the nest was made and he recognized it at once as Redtail's home. But the Redtails had not yet returned from the Sunny South, so of course that nest couldn't be occupied. He was just about to turn away when his quick ears caught the sound of quarreling voices up overhead. A moment later Mrs. Hooty arrived with more food.

So, there were young Owls up in that nest and they were living high while he, Yowler, was starving. Probably they had more than they could eat right then. He would watch his chance and when neither Hooty nor Mrs. Hooty was about he would climb up there and take what he found there, young Owls and all. He smacked his lips at the thought. So he laid his plans, and in so doing made a mistake; he neglected to plan what he would do if he should be discovered robbing that nest.

Hooty and Mrs. Hooty are good providers for their family. Yes, sir, they are good providers. They know that growing children must have plenty to eat and they make it their business to supply plenty even in times when food is scarce and hard to find. They are wonderful hunters, are Hooty and Mrs. Hooty, and they have the advantage of being able to see and hunt in both daylight and darkness. Being strong of wing they can cover a great deal of country and their hunting grounds extend far in all directions when there are babies to be fed.

So it was that often the young Owls in that nest had more than they could eat. Their parents would leave what they brought, putting it on the edge of the nest where the youngsters could get it when they wanted it. Sometimes they would quarrel over a choice bit and it would be knocked off the nest and fall to the ground. This is what had happened just before Yowler came along.

Now Yowler never had made the close acquaintance of Hooty the Owl. He knew Hooty. Of course. He had known him ever since he could remember. He had seen Hooty many times and more than once Hooty had slipped in on silent wings and snatched a Mouse or a Rabbit almost from under his very nose, but this was as far as his acquaintance with Hooty went. He had no particular respect for him. He couldn't imagine himself having respect for any bird. The idea that Hooty would dare do such a thing as attack him never had entered his mind.

However, Yowler is not by nature bold. He is always cautious and something of a sneak. He never comes out into the open if he can help himself. Even when there is no need he will do a thing in a sneaking way rather than boldly and openly. He wasn't afraid of Hooty and Mrs. Hooty, for he had had no experience with them to make him afraid. Nevertheless he preferred to do what he planned to do when they were not around. It might save some unpleasantness.

It was in the late afternoon that Yowler discovered that nest. He at once sneaked into a thicket of young hemlock trees and there hid to await the coming of the Black Shadows, for the deed he was preparing to do was a deed of darkness. From his hiding place he could watch that nest high up in a big maple. There were no branches for some distance above the ground, but Yowler knew he could climb it, and his mouth watered as he dreamed of the feast he would have once he got up there.

At last it was dusk. He saw Hooty fly off in one direction and

85

Mrs. Hooty fly off in another direction. The time had come. Sneaking out of the thicket he ran swiftly to the foot of the tree. For a moment he crouched there glaring up. Then he sprang and dug his claws into the bark and began to scramble up. As he neared the nest the young Owls heard him and took alarm. They began to hiss and snap their bills. It was a threatening sound but Yowler didn't mind it in the least. It rather amused him. He was almost there now. He could smell the uneaten food on the edge of the nest and this added to his eagerness.

And then something struck him so hard that he was almost knocked from the tree. At the same time he felt several sharp pains that made him cry out. Before he fully understood what had happened he was struck from the other side and great claws tore his coat and scratched deep gashes in his face. Snarling, spitting, Yowler tried to strike back with one claw-tipped paw while he clung to the trunk of the tree with the other. The best he could do was to rake out a few feathers. Huge wings pounded him and great claws tore his coat. He was too high up to let go and jump. He began to back down as fast as he could. Halfway he could stand it no more and simply dropped. He had lost his appetite and he had learned a lesson, a painful lesson he never would forget.

XIII. Peter Finds His Cousin Worried

In this world of strife and worry
None is wholly free from worry.

— PETER RABBIT

PETER RABBIT HAD REACHED the Green Forest without mishap. He had not had so much as one small fright. Usually he had at least one scare when crossing the Green

Meadows. Scares are a regular part of Peter's life. Having reached the Green Forest safely Peter at once began looking for his big cousin, Jumper the Hare. Jumper would be likely to know all the latest news of the Green Forest for Jumper gets about, and it is people who get about who pick up the most news.

Peter was surprised to find that hardly anywhere was there a trace of snow. Usually this early in the year there were many sheltered places in the Green Forest where banks of snow remained long after all snow had vanished from the Green Meadows. But this year gentle Sister South Wind had been very busy and her warm breath had taken away the snow faster than usual. Now there were only a very few small patches remaining here and there, and these would soon be gone.

For some time Peter ran this way and ran that way looking for his cousin, but all in vain. He was disappointed. He began to wonder if something had happened to Jumper. Could it be that Jumper had been caught by some enemy? At last Peter took to the Crooked Little Path and followed it. Finally he sat down by a tree with wide-spreading branches near the ground, a hemlock tree. There still remained a little snow beneath that tree, just a little patch. Peter merely glanced at it.

"Hello, Cousin Peter," said a voice. It sounded so near that it startled Peter. He jumped. He jumped and ran a few steps.

"Gracious, Cousin Jumper, how you scared me!" exclaimed Peter. "I didn't see you. In fact I don't see you now. Oh, yes, I do! That white coat of yours certainly makes you hard to see when you are sitting on snow. I saw that snow under the tree, but I didn't see you. Aren't you lucky to have a white coat? I wish I had one."

"No, you don't!" retorted Jumper. "You may think you do, but you don't. This white coat of mine is getting to be one of my greatest worries."

"Wha-wha-what's that?" stuttered Peter. "What do you mean it's getting to be one of your greatest worries?"

"The snow has gone too soon," explained Jumper.

"Not a bit!" declared Peter emphatically. "It couldn't go too soon for me."

"But it could for me," replied Jumper. "It has left me with a white coat."

"What of that?" demanded Peter. "What if it has?"

"How am I going to keep out of sight when there is nothing else white? Tell me that, Peter Rabbit," replied Jumper.

"Oh," said Peter a little lamely. "I hadn't thought of that. I see now what you mean. That white coat of yours does kind of show up where nothing else is white, doesn't it?"

"You see," continued Jumper, "it is worse this year than usual. It always is a worrisome time until I get my brown coat, but usually I at least begin to get it before all the snow has gone. But look at me now! Just look at me! Here is my coat still all white and the snow nearly gone. It will all be gone in a few days. As it is I have to hunt to find a patch to sit down on or beside. What I am to do when the last of the snow goes I don't know. I won't be able to move without danger of being seen by someone looking for me. I won't even be able to sit still without running the same risk. A white coat is fine in winter, but not now. No, sir, not now."

There is nothing more foolish in the world than envy. It gains no one anything, but it does make discontent and unhappiness. He who without envy rejoices in the good fortune of another is far more likely to experience good fortune himself than is one who is envious.

Most of his life Peter had been envious of his big cousin: envious because Jumper had a pure white coat in winter. When Jumper sat still on the snow it was almost impossible to see him. That is, it was almost impossible to recognize him unless you happened to know he was there. He looked like a little mound of snow and you might pass within a few feet of him without even suspecting that he was anywhere about. By simply squatting still on the snow he could be comparatively safe right out in the open. Peter had seen Hooty the Owl sail right over Jumper without seeing him just because Jumper didn't move so much as a whisker. Peter's own coat, being grayish brown, made him very easy to see against the white snow. So Peter was envious.

Together they started down the Crooked Little Path and it was plain that Jumper was nervous, very nervous indeed. Every hop or two he would stop to sit up and look all around. If a

Merry Little Breeze rustled a leaf Jumper would look anxiously this way and that way and set himself to bound away at top speed. He was afraid. There was no doubt about that. Fear was in his eyes. It showed in every movement. He was frightened half to death, as the saying is. He is naturally timid, for always hungry enemies are looking for him, but never had Peter seen him quite so anxious and worried as he now was. It made Peter himself more than usually nervous.

Peter had dropped a little behind to have a look into a hollow log off to one side of the Crooked Little Path. It was a log he had found safety in more than once. He was curious to see if anyone had been using it lately. His curiosity satisfied, he had just turned back to the Crooked Little Path when there was a loud thump. It was the danger signal from Jumper.

Away along the Crooked Little Path bounded Jumper and there behind him was Reddy Fox! Jumper left the Crooked Little Path and began to dodge among the trees. Peter watched him and gradually he began to understand why his cousin had seemed so worried. Because of that white coat Peter could see every move Jumper made, so of course Reddy Fox could too. Even when Jumper was a long way off Peter could see him, a white spot bounding now to this side and now to that. Finally Jumper disappeared over a little rise of ground, Reddy after him.

Peter remained right where he was. Just back of him was that hollow log and safety. He had only to dart into it should Reddy

Fox return. After some time, happening to glance up the hill, he saw something white under a hemlock tree. "I don't remember any snow left under that tree," thought Peter.

Even as he looked Reddy Fox came in sight headed straight for that tree. The white spot moved. It moved away from there in a hurry. It was Jumper. He had circled back as is his way sometimes. He hadn't been able to lose Reddy Fox as yet. Peter drew a long breath.

"I'm thankful," said Peter, "that my coat isn't white."

Later when Jumper returned, having rid himself of Reddy Fox, Peter admitted he was thankful.

"You should be," said Jumper.

XIV. The Home-Coming

There's no true home for bird or man
Where love has not laid out the plan.

— OLD MOTHER NATURE

THE REDTAILS, the big Hawks who for several years had made their home not far from where the Crooked Little Path winds through the Green Forest, had spent the winter far enough south to be comfortable and have good hunting. But when sweet Mistress Spring began to move northward they began to feel homesick. They wanted to get back to the Green Forest and the big nest from which they had started so many children out into the Great World with its terrible guns and ignorant killers. So they flew north with Mistress Spring and in their hurry even got a little ahead of her.

When at last they saw in the far distance the Green Forest they screamed for joy. Sailing high they swung in great circles so as to look down on all the familiar home scenes. They did not hurry to inspect the old nest. The nest was merely a part of home. It was the home scenes for which they had so longed, the Green Forest, the Green Meadows, the Smiling Pool, Laughing Brook, the Old Pasture, the Big River, the Old Orchard and, yes, Farmer Brown's home.

For a long time they circled high above all this and were filled with the great joy of home-coming. Then they set their wings to sail down to that part of the Green Forest where their nest was. It was Mrs. Redtail who first saw that all was not as it should be.

"There is someone in our nest!" she screamed indignantly, and swooped down with an angry hiss of stiff wing feathers.

Redtail was close beside her. Sure enough in that nest were two half-grown birds that they at once recognized as Owls. Mrs. Redtail swooped as if she would seize one of them and throw him from the nest, but a great brown bird with round, fierce, glaring eyes alighted on the edge of the nest with wings half spread. Mrs. Redtail changed her mind and her course abruptly and wheeled upward. Then for an hour or two angry screams and hissing and snapping of bills made that part of the Green Forest anything but pleasant. Hooty had joined Mrs.

Hooty close by the nest and together they kept guard, their heads turning with every move of the two big Hawks.

At last from sheer weariness the Redtails quit. It was useless for them to try to get their home back and they knew it. So they perched on a tall tree some distance away to rest and talk matters over. This home-coming had not been what they had thought it would be. They must make new plans.

"It is of no use," said Redtail. "Those robbers have got our home and they will keep it. We can't put them out if we try. I'm no coward, but I know when I meet someone who is too much for me."

"And that has always been such a good home," mourned Mrs. Redtail. "It is the best nest we ever had. I took a lot of pains building that nest. Yes, sir, I did so. Those robbers are too lazy to build a nest for themselves. I hate them! Yes, sir, I hate them! That is our nest and they have no right there."

Redtail stretched one of his big wings and put a couple of disarranged feathers in place. "I know how you feel, my dear," said he. "I feel much the same way. But you know the law of the Green Forest and the Green Meadows. That *was* our nest, but it isn't now. It is theirs by the law of possession. That nest was not in use and they had a right to take it."

Mrs. Redtail sighed. "Of course you are right, my dear," said she. "It is the law, and there is nothing we can do about it. We have to abide by the law, as everybody should. But, oh dear, it is such a disappointment! I had been looking forward to getting to housekeeping at once."

"I know," replied Redtail. "I never was quite so upset in my life. The question now is, what are we to do? Shall we go over to the Great Mountain to look for a place to build a new nest or shall we go farther and build in wholly new surroundings?"

Mrs. Redtail shook herself and settled her feathers. "We'll do neither," said she decidedly. "They have taken our nest, but they can't drive us from home, and the Green Forest here is really our home. We don't want those robbers for neighbors so we'll look for a tree in another part of the Green Forest and build in it. It really could be worse, you know. I guess there is nothing so bad that it couldn't be worse. I'm hungry. Let's go hunting for dinner and tomorrow we'll go look for a place to build."

During the next two days there wasn't a tree for some distance around that wasn't carefully looked over by one or the other or both. Some of the time they separated, looking in different places, and some of the time they did their looking together. Redtail found a lone pine growing in the midst of some oaks and maples. It was a big pine with wide-spreading branches and the more he looked it over the better he liked it. A little more than halfway up was a splendid crotch to support a big nest.

"I've found the tree we want!" he cried happily as he settled beside Mrs. Redtail in a big maple tree near the maple grove where every spring Farmer Brown and Farmer Brown's boy make maple syrup and maple sugar.

"No, you haven't," contradicted Mrs. Redtail.

Redtail looked surprised. "Why do you say that?" he demanded.

"Because I have found the tree we want," retorted Mrs. Redtail in her most decided manner.

"Where is it?" demanded Redtail.

"We are sitting in it," declared Mrs. Redtail.

Redtail looked the surprise he felt. He inspected the tree. "This is good, but it isn't as good as the one I have found," said he.

Mrs. Redtail pretended she hadn't heard. "We'll build right in this crotch," said she. "These two branches are perfect for holding a nest. They are too big ever to break. They are high enough yet not too high. No matter how hard the wind blows our nest will be safe."

"I'll go get the first stick right away," declared Redtail.

"The first stick is already in place. I put it there before you came," said Mrs. Redtail dryly.

Sure enough there was a fairly large stick firmly placed in that crotch. Redtail hadn't noticed it. He tried to do his share and spent much time hunting for sticks of the right size. Several times he added some to the nest when Mrs. Redtail was absent only to have her pull them out on her return. Sometimes she rearranged them and sometimes she threw them aside.

99

"That stick might do for the nest of Blacky the Crow, but not for our nest," she would say.

At last the big nest was ready to be lined. "I suppose you will be very particular about the lining," said Redtail, his eyes twinkling.

"Certainly," replied Mrs. Redtail. "I was particular about the foundation. Every stick in it is sound. I was just as particular about the smaller sticks that followed. Now for a lining I know just where I can get some nice strips of bark and I am going to use a few brown oak leaves. If you happen to find any feathers bring them along. They do make a nest look nice."

At last the nest was properly lined. Redtail looked it over critically. "Perfect," he declared.

"Not quite, my dear," replied Mrs. Redtail and flew away. In a few minutes she returned with a pine twig with its green needles. She tucked it in the side of the nest. "There," said she, "a bit of green here and there adds a lot. Suppose you bring a few more twigs like this."

Redtail chuckled and flew away. Soon he was back with a pine twig. Mrs. Redtail placed it to her satisfaction. "Yes," said she, "a touch of green adds a lot. Don't you think so?"

"Certainly, my dear. Certainly," replied Redtail and chuckled again. "There's nothing like making a good appearance."

A few more green twigs and the new home was completed. "The finest nest we ever have had," declared Redtail.

XV The Master Drummer

Politeness is of little cost;
Without it much is often lost.
— PETER RABBIT

"WHO WAS THAT DRUMMING?" demanded Peter Rabbit of his big cousin, Jumper the Hare.

"I don't hear anyone drumming," replied Jumper.

Peter listened. He didn't hear anyone drumming either. That drumming had ceased. "Well, who was it I heard drumming a few minutes ago?" demanded Peter.

"Don't you know when you hear Thunderer the Grouse?" demanded Jumper.

"It wasn't Thunderer the Grouse that I heard," replied Peter positively. "It was a different kind of drumming altogether. Someone was drumming on wood."

"Oh," replied Jumper, "it probably was one of the Woodpecker family."

"Thank you for nothing!" replied Peter a little crossly. "I knew that much. What I want to know is, which member of the Woodpecker family was it? I know the sound of most of them. This was different."

"Oh, it must be that you heard the master drummer," replied Jumper. "Now you speak of it, I remember he was drumming a little while ago."

"He is a master drummer all right; there is no doubt about that," said Peter. "But who is this master drummer?"

"Do you mean to say that you don't know the master drummer?" exclaimed Jumper. "I didn't suppose there was anyone in the Green Forest who didn't know the master drummer. You should get acquainted with him, Cousin Peter. You certainly should."

"That is what I started out to do, but when I saw you I thought you could tell me what I wanted to know," replied Peter.

"If you had kept right on the way you were heading, you probably would have soon seen him," said Jumper. "I hope you'll excuse me now, Peter, for I have an engagement. I'll see you later."

Before Peter could protest Jumper had started off and Peter knew by experience that it was quite useless for him to try to keep up with him. "Well," muttered Peter, "I suppose I may as well go on as to sit here. I wish that fellow would drum again. If he would only drum, I would be sure to find him."

But the master drummer didn't drum again. Peter would hop along a few steps, then stop to look and listen. By and by he came to the foot of a big dead tree. The ground at the foot of it was covered with chips. They were freshly cut chips. Some of them were surprisingly big chips. Peter's eyes opened very wide.

"My goodness," he muttered, "what has been going on here? It looks as if a whole party of Woodpeckers had been at work."

Peter tipped his head back and looked up. His eyes opened wider than ever. High up in that tree was a newly cut hole. It was a big hole. Yes, sir, it was a big hole. It was perfectly plain that those chips had been made by the cutting of that hole. But who could have cut a hole as big as that? Peter wanted to know. For a long time he sat staring up at the hole and then down at the chips. At last he scratched a long ear with a long hind foot. Then he scratched the other long ear with the other long hind foot. "It's too much for me," muttered Peter.

The longer Peter looked at that hole and those chips the more he was puzzled.

103

"It looks like the work of a Woodpecker," thought he, "but from the size of that hole I should say a lot of Woodpeckers must have been at work. Goldenwing the Flicker is the largest member of the Woodpecker family of my acquaintance. I have seen a lot of holes made by Goldenwing, but never in all his life has he ever cut a hole as big as this. I wonder if — "

Peter suddenly jumped right up in the air with excitement. "I do believe that this is the work of the master drummer!" he exclaimed. "Why didn't I think of that before? I'll just stay around here awhile and perhaps he may come back."

Now, Peter Rabbit is one of those fortunate people who can do about as they please. If he wants to stay awhile, he can stay awhile; if he wants to go on, he can go on. In other words, he has little to do. He has few responsibilities. The care of the children he leaves chiefly to Mrs. Peter. So now there was no reason why he shouldn't stay if he wanted to.

He found a comfortable place where he was well hidden beneath a little hemlock tree. He could peep out and see the big hole in the dead tree, and that meant that if the one who had made it returned, he would be in plain sight. After he had been sitting a little while Peter began to get sleepy. He kept dozing off. Every once in a while he would awake with a start. But at last he fell really asleep and, as there was nothing to alarm him, he slept for some time. He was awakened by the loudest rat-a-tat-tat he ever had listened to. It was so loud that it was startling. Peter's eyes flew wide open. He looked up to that big hole in the dead tree. There was no one there. Then he looked a little higher up. The drummer was there! In his surprise at the first glimpse of the drummer Peter just stared with his mouth wide open. "Why," muttered Peter, "it's Blacky the Crow! I never knew before that Blacky could drum."

Now, when Peter had first looked up, the drummer was in such a position that his head and neck were hidden. At first glance he looked to be as big as Blacky the Crow and his coat was black. So Peter's mistake was excusable. A moment later he moved so that Peter could see his head and neck. Peter realized too that this fellow wasn't quite as big as Blacky.

"It isn't Blacky, but who under the sun can it be?" muttered Peter. "My goodness, look at the red cap he wears! It stands up almost straight. It is like Sammy Jay's cap, only bigger and red. And, my goodness, what a bill! No wonder he can cut out big chips! Who under the sun can he be?"

It was true that the stranger had a surprisingly large, stout bill. What Peter called a "red cap" was really a crest of red feathers. His face and the sides of his neck were striped with white. He stretched one wing and Peter discovered that that also was barred with white. Then the stranger began to drum. He wasn't cutting out chips now. He was drumming just for the sake of hearing the noise he made. His head flew back and forth so fast that Peter's own neck ached just from watching him. And what a racket he made! Rat-a-tat-tat-tat-tat! Rat-a-tat-tat-tat-tat! The sound fairly rolled through the Green Forest. There was no doubt now in Peter's mind that he was looking at the master drummer.

XVI. Peter Gets Acquainted

A compliment will often pay
By doing much to smooth the way.
— PETER RABBIT

PETER SAT staring open-mouthed up at the master drummer. As he recovered from his surprise he began to do a little thinking.

"That fellow is a Woodpecker," thought Peter. "Yes, sir, he is a member of the Woodpecker family. He has to be. He couldn't have a head and bill like that and not be a Wood-pecker. He couldn't cling to the trunk of a tree like that and not be a Woodpecker. He couldn't drum like that and not be a Woodpecker. But I didn't suppose there was any member of the Woodpecker family as big as that fellow. I must get acquainted with him. Yes, sir, I must get acquainted with him."

Peter hopped out from under the little hemlock tree where he had been sitting. When the master drummer paused for breath, Peter thumped as hard as he could with his long hind feet. The stranger looked down.

"Good morning, Longears," said the stranger. "Or do you prefer to be called Longlegs?"

"I don't like to be called either," replied Peter with dignity. "My name is Peter Rabbit, if you please. You may call me Peter."

"Thank you," replied the stranger with a twinkle in his eyes. "How do you do this morning, Peter?"

"I'm feeling fine, thank you," replied Peter most politely. "How are you feeling yourself?"

"Never felt better in my life," replied the stranger. "The better I feel, the better I can drum. Listen to this."

The stranger's head flew back and forth so fast that Peter could hardly see it, and through the Green Forest rang that rat-a-tat-tat-tat which had brought Peter over there. "How is that?" asked the stranger when he had paused for breath.

"Wonderful!" replied Peter. "Wonderful! Never in all my life have I heard such drumming."

The stranger looked pleased. "That was nothing," said he. "Listen to this." Once more that red-crested head of his flew back and forth and once more the Green Forest fairly rang with the noise. When he stopped drumming Peter hastened to repeat that it was wonderful.

"You haven't told me yet who you are," Peter ventured at last.

"I'm a Woodpecker," replied the stranger.

"I thought you must be," said Peter. "In fact, I almost knew that you are a cousin of Goldenwing the Flicker and Downy and Hairy, the Woodpecker cousins. But I don't believe I know your name. I don't remember ever having heard of any member of the Woodpecker family as big as you. Are you the biggest of the family?"

The stranger shook his head. "No," said he, "I am not the biggest. There is one other bigger than I. His name is Ivory Bill. You won't see him around here though. He lives down in the Sunny South where few people ever see him. I would feel small beside him."

"Goodness!" exclaimed Peter. "He must be a big fellow. If you please, why do they call him Ivory Bill?"

"Because," replied the stranger, "he has a big white bill. So they call him Ivory Bill. Excuse me, Peter, I just must drum. When I feel like drumming I just have to drum." Suiting action to the word, the master drummer began once more to beat out his wonderful rat-a-tat-tat-tat.

"If you please, Mr. Drummer," said Peter, when he got a chance, "you haven't told me your name yet."

"Haven't I?" exclaimed the stranger. "Now that's too bad. I am the Pileated Woodpecker. Some folks call me Logcock; some folks call me Black Cock-of-the-Woods. You can take your choice."

"Do you know what?" asked Peter.

"What?" replied the big Woodpecker.

"I don't like either of those names," explained Peter. "I'm going to call you something different."

"What?" demanded the stranger.

"I am going to call you Master Drummer, for that is just what you are," replied Peter.

The big Woodpecker looked pleased. He was pleased. "All right," said he, "that suits me."

"By the way, what does Pileated mean?" inquired Peter.

"That's a fair question," replied the other. "Pileated means crested. You see what a big, red crest I have. So they call me the Pileated Woodpecker."

"I should think it would be a lot simpler and more sensible to call you just the Crested Woodpecker," said Peter. "By the way, did you make that big hole?"

Just then who should come along but Jumper the Hare "Hello, Peter!" exclaimed Jumper. "I see you found Logcock, the master drummer."

"Yes," replied Peter. "Do you call him Logcock?"

Jumper nodded. "Everybody around here who knows him calls him Logcock," said he.

"I've told him that I'm going to call him Master Drummer," replied Peter.

"That's very good," replied Jumper, "but I guess he'll be Logcock to the rest of us. How about it, Logcock?"

The big Woodpecker nodded. "I've answered to that name so long," said he, "that I guess I always will."

"Is Mrs. Logcock around?" inquired Jumper.

"No," replied Logcock, "but I hope she will arrive soon. She must have heard me drumming. I presume she is over on the Great Mountain where I left her, but I think she can hear me drumming way up there."

"Have you decided to stay in the Green Forest?" said Peter.

"That all depends on Mrs. Logcock," was the reply. "What she says goes. If she doesn't come soon, I shall have to go to look for her."

"I hope you'll find her and that you'll both stay here," said Peter.

"Thank you, Peter," replied Logcock.

"Why haven't I ever seen you over here in the Green Forest before this?" asked Peter.

"Probably because I've only been here for very brief visits in the past," replied Logcock. "I've been living over on the Great Mountain."

"It's very nice over here in the Green Forest," said Peter.

"So I've discovered," replied Logcock. "It is so very nice that if I can get Mrs. Logcock down here, I am quite sure we will stay. Hello! I think I hear a familiar voice."

Peter listened. Before he had made quite certain that he heard anything unusual, Logcock opened his mouth and sent out a call that was familiar, yet not familiar. It was something like the call of Goldenwing the Flicker, but was louder, clearer and sharper. As he finished it Logcock turned his head to one side that he might listen better. Almost at once he got a reply. Peter heard it this time.

"She is coming," said Logcock, looking down at Peter.

"Who is coming?" demanded Peter.

"Mrs. Logcock," was the reply.

Peter began to get a little excited. Presently he caught sight of a black form above the treetops. Logcock called again and a moment later Mrs. Logcock lighted on the tree on which Logcock had been drumming. She looked very much like Logcock. In fact, Peter thought she looked just like him until he discovered that Logcock's red crest went clear down across his forehead to the beginning of his bill, while Mrs. Logcock's red crest went only part way. Then, too, Logcock had a patch of red running back from each corner of his bill, while Mrs. Logcock did not.

Such a bowing and bobbing as there was on the part of Logcock! Peter had never seen anything like it. "I'm so glad you've come, my dear," said Logcock.

"Huh!" replied Mrs. Logcock. "If you are so glad, why didn't you come to get me?"

"I was just about to, my dear, I was just about to," replied Logcock. "I think we'll make our home here."

"If there is any thinking to be done, I'll do it," replied Mrs. Logcock rather ungraciously. It was plain that she was somewhat out of sorts because Logcock had left her alone up on the Great Mountain. And it was also plain that she didn't intend to be pleased with anything that Logcock suggested. It didn't take him long to find this out. So he suggested that they go back to the Great Mountain to make their home. Mrs. Logcock had no intention of agreeing with him in anything, so now she declared that, having come so far, she proposed to look over the Green Forest thoroughly and perhaps they would make their home there. Down inside Logcock chuckled. He knew that the matter was as good as settled. He knew that Mrs. Logcock had made up her mind to stay. As he had already made up his mind, that was all there was to it.

XVII. The Eyes of Love

On earth below, in skies above
The keenest eyes are those of love.

— OLD MOTHER NATURE

GO WHERE YOU WILL you will find that that saying holds
true. Not only are the eyes of love the keenest but they also are
the quickest and the most understanding. No other eyes in all
the Great World are as watchful.

Two pairs of keen eyes were watching Thunderer the Grouse
as he drummed and strutted on a mossy old log just off the
Crooked Little Path. After Thunderer had drummed with his
wings the long roll that sounded like distant thunder, he would

stand very still with head stretched high, looking and listening. None knew better than he that many ears other than those for whom his drumming was intended had been listening. Very likely some belonged to hungry hunters with a liking for Grouse dinners. So his sharp eyes would search his surroundings and his keen ears would be set to catch every faintest sound.

After a wait he would strut, displaying his lovely black ruff and spreading fanwise his beautiful tail with its border of a wide band of black between two narrow bands of gray. Sometimes he would be so intent on showing off to the very best of his ability that he would forget to watch for enemies. His keen eyes would glance this way and that searching for Mrs. Grouse, his ladylove, and they were blind to all else. It was at one such time that Reddy Fox crawled and wiggled forward a wee bit, his eyes fixed on Thunderer so as to stop the instant the latter stopped strutting.

Mrs. Grouse, hidden and unseen by either Thunderer or Reddy, watched every move that Thunderer made. "There is no one like him. He is the most wonderful bird that ever lived. Was ever there another so handsome? And he's doing that all for me," said she to herself.

Now her eyes were the eyes of love. Because of this she saw how Thunderer forgot to keep watch while he was strutting, so she kept watch for him. Despite the fact that she wanted to keep her eyes on him every second she looked this way and she looked that way every time Thunderer strutted. Between his drumming and his strutting, when he stood so alert and watchful, she didn't worry about him. She knew that then no enemy, however stealthy and clever, could steal unseen near enough to catch him. But when he was so taken up with his strutting she felt that she should be eyes for him, and unknown to him she was.

So it happened that as she glanced this way and that way she thought she saw something move. Perhaps it was just some leaves on the ground stirred by the passing of one of Mother West Wind's children, the Merry Little Breezes. She looked hard at that spot when she wanted to be looking at Thunderer. Yes, something did move there and it wasn't a leaf. Thunderer still strutted back and forth along the mossy old log, but she didn't so much as glance at him.

He stopped strutting and once more was the alert watcher. Nothing moved in the place on which Mrs. Grouse kept her eyes fixed. After a while Thunderer drummed. At the end of it he stood as before, still, alert, watchful, even suspicious. For a long time he stood so. Then, satisfied that all was well and no enemy was near, he began to strut again. At once Mrs. Grouse saw something move. For a few minutes she couldn't make out what it was. Then suddenly she saw what it was.

"Reddy Fox!" she exclaimed under her breath. She watched him wiggle along as close to the ground as he could get. He was trying to get unseen to a fallen tree from behind which he might be able to make a successful rush and leap. She looked over at Thunderer. He was strutting his very best.

"The poor foolish dear," she thought. "What would he do without me? He hasn't the least idea that Reddy Fox is around."

At last Reddy reached the fallen tree. Behind it he crept along until he could peek around. There he waited until once more Thunderer started to strut. Cautiously Reddy set himself for a swift rush and leap.

There was a startling roar. It was made by the stout wings of Mrs. Grouse as she whirred away among the trees. Instantly there was a second roar and Thunderer had left the mossy old log in full flight. Even then he didn't know what the danger was.

Love does foolish things and mean things because it is jealous without cause. It is suspicious and quarrelsome. It is boastful and vain. And it is the most wonderful thing in all the Great World.

Thunderer was again drumming with his stout wings as he stood on the end of the mossy old log. He didn't know where Mrs. Grouse was but he was sure that she was within hearing. This drumming was a message to her to let her know that he was thinking of her, that she was his ladylove, and for her sake he would dare all things. It was a call to her, but at the same time it was a warning to all others who might hear it that he was ready, even eager, to fight for her. So it was a call and a challenge.

Early each morning Thunderer drummed and after each drumming he listened for a reply. Day after day there was none. Then one morning as he stood listening he heard a long roll of distant thunder. His eyes flashed with anger. Another Grouse

had dared to answer his challenge. Thunderer waited a few minutes and all the time his anger grew. Then he drummed a reply. He warned the unknown stranger that he was an intruder where he had no business to be, and that if he knew what was good for himself he would go away and stay away.

There was no immediate reply. Satisfied that the intruder had heeded his warning Thunderer began to strut. He wasn't sure that Mrs. Grouse was watching him, but he hoped she was and he had a feeling that she was. So he strutted as he had never strutted before. Right in the midst of it came that low rolling thunder again. It seemed to mock him and it certainly did challenge him. That the drummer was bold and unafraid was clear in the very sound. It put an abrupt end to Thunderer's strutting. Who could this upstart be who dared so boldly to reply to his challenge? Thunderer drummed again and immediately there was a reply. Thunderer couldn't wait for the intruder to come to him. Perhaps despite his boldness he wouldn't come. So Thunderer started to look for him.

He knew every good drumming log and other drumming place in that part of the Green Forest. The bold stranger must be using one of them and Thunderer thought he knew which one it was. He bristled with anger as he hurried in search of his rival.

Now of course Mrs. Grouse had heard all that drumming and she understood what it all meant. She had been watching Thunderer, all the time taking care that he didn't get so much as a glimpse of her. Now she was pleasurably excited. She wondered who the newcomer was. She wondered if he was as big and handsome as Thunderer. She wanted to see him. Perhaps there would be a fight. If so it would be over and because of her. What a thrill that would be! What if after all Thunderer should be beaten and driven away! It was unthinkable, yet such things did happen. And what a Grouse it would be who could defeat Thunderer! She must be there to see.

There was another who heard and understood that drumming. It was Reddy Fox. He had tried and failed to catch Thunderer on his drumming log because Mrs. Grouse had given warning. But here was another drummer who might not be as smart as Thunderer, and who might have no one to warn him. And supposing those two Grouse got to fighting! What a chance that would be! Reddy decided to try again for a Grouse dinner to take home to Mrs. Reddy and the cubs.

XVIII. A Fight for a Lady

A coward he, possessed by fear,
Who will not fight for those held dear.
—OLD MOTHER NATURE

BRISTLING WITH ANGER, jealous anger, Thunderer cautiously, quietly approached a certain old drumming log that he no longer used, but which he still considered to be his own. On it stood a Grouse whom he never had seen before. He had just drummed a challenge to fight and was now standing very straight with his head held high, the crest slightly raised and his ruff spread. He was listening for a reply.

This stranger was big, quite as big as Thunderer himself. He was handsome, too. And he was young, filled with the eagerness and confidence of youth. Jealousy filled the heart of Thunderer. Yes, sir, jealousy filled his heart and all in an instant that jealousy became hate. It is a strange thing how quickly jealousy can turn to hate. So, because jealousy so often springs from love and then becomes hate, we see something dreadful springing from something very beautiful, for hate is always dreadful, while there is nothing more beautiful than love.

Thunderer stepped out into the open and the handsome young Grouse saw him. At almost the same instant both saw Mrs. Grouse peeping out from some brush, watching them. That was like a spark that sets off an explosion. Instantly they were at each other, striking with stout bills and feet. Feathers flew. This was a fight for a lady and there would be no quarter. Of course the lady was Mrs. Grouse. Perhaps her heart was really Thunderer's all the time. Perhaps she wasn't sure of this, and only as a result of this fight could she be sure one way or the other. Anyway it was exciting and flattering to be fought for by two such brave and handsome rivals. Thunderer was a dear, and so handsome and brave. But his rival was just as handsome and just as brave. He was younger and she wasn't sure that he wasn't handsomer. She would be sorry to see him whipped and driven away. Or would she? It is difficult for a lady to know her own heart when she is being fought for by two handsome rivals.

Meanwhile the fighters forgot everything but their hate for each other. They even forgot Mrs. Grouse. They forgot that they were fighting for a lady. They forgot that there was anyone but themselves in all the Great World. Of course that included their enemies.

So they dashed at each other and tumbled about on the dry leaves and struck savagely with beaks and claws. The feathers flew. It was a thrilling yet a sorry sight. Now and then they stopped for breath and a moment of rest, but not once did they take their eyes from each other. Thunderer was perhaps a wee bit the heavier, but he wasn't quite so quick as the other. The other possessed the quickness of youth. But what Thunderer may have lacked in quickness he made up for in the cunning of long experience. He was wary and clever, and knew how to protect himself while watching for a chance to strike. He had fought and won many such battles. It had happened every spring since he could remember.

"It is just like old times," thought Mrs. Grouse as she looked on. She looked at Thunderer fondly. "He is fighting for me just as hard as he did when we first met."

Then she looked at the other. "How quick he is! He is wonderful!" she exclaimed under her breath. There was admiration in her eyes as she watched him.

The news of that fight traveled fast. Such news usually does. In a surprisingly short time several pairs of eyes besides those of Mrs. Grouse were looking on. Blacky the Crow was there. So was Sammy Jay. Chatterer the Red Squirrel was barking encouragement to both fighters and in his excitement running up and down the trunk of a tree. There were others.

All these were harmless spectators. But other ears had heard the drumming of the rivals, the keen ears of Reddy Fox. Knowing the ways of the Grouse folk he had been sure that a fight would follow. He would try again for a dinner for Mrs. Reddy and the cubs. He is not the kind to be discouraged by one disappointment or two. Long ago he learned that nothing is lost by trying over and over again.

First he went to the mossy old log on which he had seen Thunderer drum and strut. Thunderer wasn't there. Reddy grinned. "He has gone to look for that other drummer and I think I know where," thought he.

Moving with the greatest care not to rustle a dry leaf or step on a dead twig and make it snap, he reached the edge of a small opening among the trees. In the middle of it was a sight to gladden the eyes of a hungry Fox, two big birds fighting.

"I could walk right up to them and they wouldn't see me," thought he, but he didn't try it. He would take no chance that Blacky the Crow or Sammy Jay might see him and give the alarm. Perhaps those fighters would tumble and roll over his way. Instead they gradually moved the other way. Stealthily Reddy crept around toward the other side. In a moment he would be near enough.

That moment never came. From almost beneath his very nose

there was a startling roar of wings. So close were they that they almost brushed his nose. Mrs. Grouse whirred across that little opening and up into a tree. Before Reddy could recover from his startled surprise Thunderer had roared up to join her, and his rival had whirred away as if he had an important engagement elsewhere.

"I hope he won't come back," said Mrs. Grouse. He didn't.

So within two days Thunderer had twice been saved by Mrs. Grouse. From then on they never were far apart. Sometimes Thunderer drummed for her admiration, or from sheer joy, or to warn any possible rivals within hearing that they would not be allowed in the neighborhood. Often he strutted magnificently to show Mrs. Grouse what a handsome and important mate was hers. She no longer looked on secretly but openly showed her admiration. He was most attentive to her and together they roamed about their chosen part of the Green Forest and were filled with the joy of spring and with the company of each other.

Came a time when now and then Mrs. Grouse would slip away for a while. At first Thunderer didn't notice this. He was too busy trying to show his own importance to notice much else. Self-important people are like this. But after a few days Thunderer became aware that often Mrs. Grouse was not near when he looked for approval. He spoke to her about it.

"Where have you been?" he asked.

"Not far," replied Mrs. Grouse demurely. "My dear, you never looked handsomer than you do this minute."

At once Thunderer began to strut, all else forgotten. The next day he missed her again. She was gone longer than before. When he wanted to know where she had been she changed the subject. He began watching her, but she would slip away while his head was turned. One instant she would be beside him and the next instant she would be gone.

Thunderer became suspicious. Why did she leave him that way? He became jealous, but of whom or what he didn't know. Suspicion is like that. He tried to keep watch of her but she continued to fool him. It was annoying. It was exasperating. She was so secretive that after a while he suspected that she was hiding something from him. He accused her of having a secret which she was keeping from him.

"Yes," admitted Mrs. Grouse, "I have a secret. It is a very nice secret, a perfectly wonderful secret."

"What is it?" demanded Thunderer crossly.

"You'll know some day," replied Mrs. Grouse sweetly. A few minutes later she disappeared.

XIX. The Secret That Was Kept

If you must boast take care that you
Tell what you've done, not what you'll do.

— OLD MOTHER NATURE

"DO YOU THINK it is right to have a secret from your own mate?" demanded Thunderer crossly.

"Of course, or I wouldn't have one. It is that kind of a secret," replied Mrs. Grouse.

"There isn't any such kind of secret," retorted Thunderer sharply.

"Yes, there is," replied Mrs. Grouse sweetly. "It is a secret too precious for me to share with anyone, even you. A secret is twice as safe with one as with two, and some secrets are so precious that it is wrong to take a chance. Sharing it with another is taking a chance. This is one of that kind."

Just then Thunderer remembered something. He remembered that in other springs Mrs. Grouse had acted just this way and later he had learned why. "I know your secret!" he cried triumphantly. "You have a nest!"

"Yes," admitted Mrs. Grouse, "I have a nest, but that isn't the real secret."

Thunderer gave no heed to this. "I knew it!" he cried. "Where is it?"

"That," replied Mrs. Grouse, "is the secret."

"Why won't you tell me where it is? Don't you think I should know? After all it is my nest too, isn't it?" said Thunderer.

Mrs. Grouse shook her head. "No, no, no. That is the answer for all three questions," she declared. "I won't tell you where it is for the reason already stated. I don't think you should know because I am afraid you might be jealous of it for taking so much of my time away from you. And it isn't your nest anyway; I made it."

"Are there eggs in it?" asked Thunderer.

"That also is no business of yours," retorted Mrs. Grouse.

"Which means that there are eggs there," replied Thunderer knowingly. "I guess I can find that nest if I really want to."

"Then don't want to, because I don't want you to," said Mrs. Grouse. Then she added mischievously, "If you do find it you will be smarter than you've ever been before."

"You don't trust me," said Thunderer.

"True," replied Mrs. Grouse. "I don't trust anyone but myself, and sometimes I don't really trust myself."

"Is the nest near here?" asked Thunderer artlessly as he pretended to be very busy scratching among the leaves. Receiving no answer he looked around. Mrs. Grouse was nowhere in sight. His keen eyes searched the surroundings. He listened for the rustle of dry leaves under moving feet. He looked and he listened in vain.

"She thinks she can fool me, but she can't. I'll show her," muttered Thunderer. "I'll find that nest and I'll break it up. That's what I'll do. Then perhaps she will stay with me."

And that is just what Mrs. Grouse was afraid he would do.

"The poor dear doesn't like it because I leave him alone so much. He is jealous of this nest and these eggs because they keep me away from him so much. That is silly, but it is so. If he should know where they are it would be just like him to break them up," thought she.

She was right. Thunderer in the pride of his fine appearance liked to strut and show what a handsome fellow he was, but there is no satisfaction in strutting with none to see and admire and he wanted to be admired. So he was peeved because Mrs. Grouse no longer stayed around to admire him and he was peeved that she should keep a secret from him. He made up his mind that he would find that nest. He boasted that he would.

Now it is foolish to boast at any time, but to boast of what you will do, not what you have done, is the height of foolishness.

131

Thunderer was finding this out. He had looked and looked but all his looking had proved in vain.

Mrs. Grouse would join him each day for a short time and together they would search for tender new grass and other green things, and for bugs and worms and insects. Sometimes when his back was turned Mrs. Grouse would silently slip away. Sometimes she would suddenly take to her wings. When she did this Thunderer would follow only to have her disappear behind some thick growth where she would go to ground, run swiftly, and be hidden in the underbrush by the time he arrived.

Once Thunderer walked past that nest within little more than a foot of it without even suspecting he was near it. Mrs. Grouse had seen him coming. Quickly she had reached out and picked up a number of old dead brown leaves. These she had placed on her back. Then she had slipped off the nest, the leaves sliding down her back and tail and off over the eggs. Silently but swiftly she had run a short distance, then squatted behind a tree. Thunderer had passed without seeing her or the eggs. Fooling him was a sort of game. I suspect that she rather enjoyed it.

So day by day Thunderer became more and more discomfited, and more and more peeved. But there was nothing he could do about it. While he wouldn't have admitted it to anyone else he had to admit to himself that Mrs. Grouse was too smart for him.

That nest was on the ground. It was a slight hollow lined with dead leaves. In it were ten eggs. They filled it. It would be a little over three weeks until those eggs hatched. All that long time they must be kept warm and hidden from sharp eyes of folks with an appetite for eggs. Blacky the Crow was one. Sammy Jay was another. Chatterer the Red Squirrel is a great egg hunter. There was Jimmy Skunk and there was Reddy Fox. She knew that Reddy would like nothing better than to get the eggs and herself as well. And there were others. All those sharp-eyed folk must be fooled if there was to be a family of little Grouse.

Now no one knows better than does Mrs. Grouse how perfectly her coat blends with the brown leaves and needles and sticks covering the ground. So when she was ready to make a nest she had looked until she found a place at the foot of an old stump where the ground was well covered with these things. It was partly shaded and protected from above by a low spreading branch of a young hemlock tree. There she scratched out a slight hollow and lined it with leaves, brown dead leaves of which so many were scattered about. When the ten eggs had been laid she began the long lone task of sitting on them for twenty-four days, leaving them only to get her food. Eggs or no eggs, she must eat. When she left them she first took great care to make sure that no one was about to see her leave. Then she covered the precious eggs with leaves.

Comfortably settled on her eggs Mrs. Grouse seemed to be a part of her surroundings. Only her bright watchful eyes seemed alive. Do you think it didn't require courage to sit there day after day, night after night, knowing that at any moment a hungry hunter might appear?

One evening as the moonlight came stealing in among the

trees, making patches of light and deep shadows, Mrs. Grouse saw something white in the very middle of a place so dark that it seemed black, and it moved. Instantly she was wide-awake. She kept her eyes on that moving spot of white. It moved this way and that and at last out into the moonlight stepped Jimmy Skunk.

"I thought so," said Mrs. Grouse to herself. "I hope he won't come this way."

He did come that way. He didn't come directly or quickly. Perhaps the strain would have been easier to bear if he had. Anyway it would have been over sooner. Jimmy just wandered about this way and that, stopping at an old stump to dig around it, pausing to pull over a stick, scraping the leaves out from a little hollow between the roots of a tree. Jimmy was hunting for fat beetles and grubs and other crawling folk who live in such places.

Supposing he should come poking around this stump so close to her? Mrs. Grouse shivered at the thought. Jimmy came nearer and nearer. It took courage to sit there watching, waiting, hardly breathing. And when he went around behind that old stump and she could hear him digging between the roots there it required even more courage to keep still. But she did it and Jimmy didn't find her.

XX. Mrs. Grouse Holds Her Breath

Don't underrate another lest
You find yourself but second best.
— OLD MOTHER NATURE

REDDY FOX WAS over in the Green Forest. Mrs. Grouse
saw him on the Crooked Little Path when he was some distance
away. Should she cover her eggs with leaves and steal away to

safety? The temptation was great. Twice she started to do it, then settled back. She couldn't, just couldn't, leave those precious eggs. In a week they would hatch. If she left them and Reddy should find them nothing could be done to save them. Even if she remained she might not be able to save them but she could try. If he should see her she could pretend to be hurt. She could flop along the ground as if she had a broken wing and couldn't fly. Thus she might lead him away from her treasures. It was an old trick she had used successfully with other Foxes.

Very handsome Reddy looked as he came down the Crooked Little Path. His black ears were set to catch the faintest sounds, the squeak of a Mouse or the rustle of dry leaves by careless little feet. He stopped to look, listen and smell, lifting his black nose to sift out all the scents brought by the Merry Little Breezes, children of Old Mother West Wind. It was that wonderful nose that Mrs. Grouse feared most.

He drew nearer. Mrs. Grouse flattened herself on the nest and drew down her feathers tightly to keep in all body scent. Right in front of her he sat down back to her. He was so near she could almost have pecked his bushy tail. She held her breath. In a few minutes he moved on. She breathed freely again. Hardly was he out of sight when Chatterer the Red Squirrel appeared.

As all the feathered folks know, Chatterer has a liking for eggs. Come spring that liking becomes a longing that must be satisfied. Anyway he thinks it must. Have you noticed that when you want something very much you soon get the feeling that you must have it? That you can't get along without it?

So Chatterer spent much time these days watching his feathered neighbors, hoping thus to find out where they had built or were building nests. Long ago he found out that often the quickest and easiest way to find a nest is to watch the owners of it. It was by chance that he caught a glimpse of Mrs. Grouse over in the Green Forest. The sight of her reminded him of the greatest feast of eggs he had ever had when once on a time he had been lucky enough to find the nest of a Grouse. There were more eggs than he could eat at one time, so he had two meals that he never had forgotten.

"I wonder," said Chatterer, "if she has a nest now. If she hasn't she probably will have soon. A nest full of her eggs would be worth more than all the eggs in all the nests in the Old Orchard. Ah, there's Mr. Grouse, old Thunderer himself! The vain old strutter! He certainly has a good opinion of himself."

He watched Thunderer for a moment, then turned to look at Mrs. Grouse. She wasn't where he had seen her only a moment before. He thought she had stepped behind a tree or stump or clump of ferns. He looked back at Thunderer. He was still showing off and Chatterer knew it was for the admiration of Mrs. Grouse. "She wouldn't leave while he is doing that," thought Chatterer.

That was his mistake. He didn't know Mrs. Grouse as well as he thought he did. That was the very time Mrs. Grouse would and did slip away. "She has hidden her nest and she probably has a lot of eggs now and has begun sitting on them," thought he. "I'll be around here tomorrow at this time and I'll watch her. She may fool old Thunderer, but not me. No, sir, she won't fool me again."

That was an idle boast. He saw her the next morning and he lost her just as he had before, only this time it wasn't because he watched Thunderer. He was sure that he didn't take his eyes off Mrs. Grouse. To be sure as she moved about feeding she did now and then go out of sight for an instant as she went behind a tree or a bit of brush or an old log. He was sure that he knew right where she was all the time, yet somehow she had stolen away. It was provoking.

"If only I can see her and not be seen by her she may show me what I can't find for myself," said he.

At last he did see her and she didn't see him. At least that is what he thought.

He was lying flat along a limb of a tree from which he could keep watch for quite a distance in all directions. Mrs. Grouse came in sight walking cautiously with her head held high and her keen black eyes looking this way and that way. She was the image of suspicion. Chatterer grinned. She began scratching among the leaves, now and then picking up something, just what he could not see. She found some tender green plants that were to her liking. Now and then she stopped, straightened up and stood still, looking and listening.

After a while she moved away quite as if going nowhere in particular, just wandering about, but Chatterer noticed that she was more watchful than ever, turning her head quickly to look keenly this way and that way. Now and then she pretended to pick up something as if she were not yet through feeding. Chatterer chuckled. Then as Mrs. Grouse was getting where she would soon be lost to sight he cautiously followed by way of the treetops. He was very cute about it. He kept out of sight as best he could, showing himself only when passing from one tree to another by the overhead route where the branches were slender and there was nothing to hide behind. He watched Mrs. Grouse sharply then and he was sure that not once did she see him.

This was fun. He was enjoying every minute of it. It usually is fun to prove oneself smarter than someone else. So Chatterer was enjoying it and at the same time in his mind was already eating those eggs he was sure he would soon really have.

Mrs. Grouse became more and more cautious, or seemed to. She approached a small balsam tree. Just beyond it and close to it was an old stump, a big stump. She stood for what seemed to Chatterer a long time looking about suspiciously. Then quickly she slipped under the balsam tree. She disappeared and she didn't reappear on the other side.

Chatterer grinned. "Her nest is under that little green tree," thought he.

He ran down to the ground and circled around so as to reach that old stump from the other side. His claws rattled on the wood as he dug them in. Mrs. Grouse burst out from beneath the little balsam tree with a roar of wings and whirred away. Chatterer chuckled. He had hoped she would do just that. He

140

had planned to startle her so that she would fly and leave those eggs unprotected.

"Now I'll find out!" he cried happily as he ran down the stump to search under the little balsam tree.

He did find out, but not until he had hunted long and carefully. Then it wasn't what he had expected to find out. He didn't find out where that nest was, but he did find out that it wasn't there. Then he flew into a rage. He knew that Mrs. Grouse had seen him after all.

XXI. Anxious Happiness

None to himself alone may live;
Unconsciously we take and give.
— MRS. GROUSE

MRS. GROUSE, SITTING on her ten precious eggs, watched the first Jolly Little Sunbeams drive the Black Shadows out of the Green Forest. She had watched the same thing many times since the last of those eggs was laid. Many days had passed, all much alike, days of patience, watchfulness, pleasant dreaming, anxious suspense. This day, the twenty-fourth day of her sitting there, would be different. She knew it the instant she opened her eyes before the first Jolly Little Sunbeam appeared. This was *the* day.

Beneath the feathers of her breast there was a small stir. She changed her position so as to look down at the eggs just there. There was a hole in one of them and even as she looked the egg moved. Her heart sang. Yes, this was *the* day, *hatching* day. It was the day of reward for patience and courage and clever outwitting of enemies.

She settled down again, her feathers fluffed and spread to cover every one of those eggs which before this day was over would be but empty shells. The last of the Black Shadows had been driven out and the golden light of early morning flooded through the Green Forest. Never had it been more lovely. Not far away Melody the Wood Thrush was pouring out his love in exquisite song. His vesper song had been the last thing Mrs. Grouse heard the evening before.

In the distance Blacky the Crow cawed and was answered by Mrs. Blacky. Somehow their voices didn't sound as harsh as usual. From under a small balsam tree Jumper the Hare hopped out. He had changed from his white winter coat to his brown summer coat. He hopped past not three feet from Mrs. Grouse without suspecting her nearness. Mrs. Grouse chuckled a silent little chuckle and watched him out of sight.

There were more stirrings beneath her and her happiness increased until it was so great as to be almost painful. Her long vigil was almost at an end. After today she would no longer have to sit hour after hour, peacefully enough most of the time it is true, but at other times holding her breath in dread suspense lest a hungry enemy discover her.

There was a faint thump from beyond where Jumper the Hare had disappeared. That was his danger signal. She knew it as well as if she were a member of his family. A moment later Jumper came in sight. He was running in easy jumps. Just in front of her he stopped and sat up to look back. A sharp, crafty face appeared. It was Reddy Fox. Jumper stamped hard, turned and was away. This time he was hurrying.

Mrs. Grouse paid no heed to Jumper. Her eyes were fixed on Reddy. Supposing he should find her now? Why couldn't he have kept away for just one more day? What should she do? Should she continue to sit tight, or should she slip off the nest and show herself, pretending to be hurt so that Reddy would try to catch her and she could lead him away, always keeping just out of his reach?

The question was decided for her. Blacky the Crow decided it. He lighted on the top of the stump behind her. He could look right down on her, and there are no sharper eyes than those of Blacky the Crow. He didn't look down. He saw Reddy Fox. They are old rivals in the search for food and neither loves the other.

"Caw, caw, caw!" shrieked Blacky. To all the Green Forest folk who heard it it meant "Fox, Fox, Fox!"

Reddy looked up at Blacky and showed all his teeth. Then he turned and trotted away. It was useless for him to try to hunt there with Blacky around. Blacky continued to caw jeeringly until Reddy was out of sight, then spread his black wings and went on about his own business.

Late that afternoon a proud but anxious mother brooded ten of the prettiest babies in all the Great World, ten brown, downy, wee chicks that soon would follow her from that nest to which neither she nor they ever would return.

Not in all the Green Forest could you have found a more anxious person than Mrs. Grouse. Neither could you have found a happier one. It is curious how anxiety and happiness so often go together, and how often the increase of one is accompanied by an increase of the other. Just how this is none but mothers know.

Sitting on her eggs for twenty-four long days Mrs. Grouse had had many anxious moments and much happiness in keeping her treasures warm and protected. But the worries of those days were nothing to the anxieties of the present, nor was the happiness of those days to be compared with the happiness she now knew. You see she was now a mother, the mother of ten of the dearest, prettiest, liveliest babies you can imagine.

Every one of her eggs had hatched. That in itself was a cause for happiness and at the same time for worry. You see each one of those wee chicks was a separate and individual worry. Had some of those eggs failed to hatch there would have been just so many fewer worries. When those chicks were just eggs she could leave them to get her food. Now they couldn't be left. Where she went they must go too. She must see that they kept with her, and not only must she find food for herself but until they were old enough to find their own food she must find it for them.

Very proud was Mrs. Grouse when she led her family from the nest at the foot of an old stump. Now she didn't care who found it for it was no longer home. Where was home? For the babies home was where Mother was. In fact Mother herself was home for them for it was under her protecting wings that they would spend many nights, and it was there that they would find warmth and shelter when they were cold or wet. Mother was home. Yes, sir, Mother was home.

She had been a most cautious and watchful person when she was only the keeper of precious eggs. That was nothing to what she was now. Those bright eyes of hers did not miss the movement of a single leaf within their vision. Those keen ears of hers, hidden though they were by feathers, didn't miss the faintest sound though it were no more than two leaves whispering together. Yet she did not for an instant lose sight of one of those ten babies. At the first sound that seemed to her the least bit suspicious she clucked a warning of which they seemed unaware as their busy little feet ran this way and that over the warm earth and the brown leaves. They were aware of it, how-

ever, for if it was followed by a certain rather sharp call that meant "Hide!" they disappeared all in a second.

The way in which they obeyed that hide signal was something to see. Yes, sir, it was something to see. One instant they were running about. The next instant you wouldn't have guessed that there was one anywhere around. The instant they heard that alarm each darted under cover, some under leaves, some under sticks, some into small holes or hollows, and there each kept still. How did each know just where to go? You tell. Perhaps when they heard that first warning and seemed to pay no attention to it each really was looking for the nearest place to hide should it become necessary.

How had Mother taught them all this in so short a time? She hadn't. The knowledge of what to do had been born in them just as had the knowledge of how to walk and run. They hadn't had to learn how to use their little legs. There is a name for all such knowledge. It is called instinct. It is the impulse to do certain things without conscious thought. It is Mother Nature's means of protecting her otherwise helpless children of the Green Forest and the Green Meadows.

So began the most anxious time yet the happiest time for Mrs. Grouse. As for Thunderer, he knew the secret now and he was almost as proud of those chicks as was their mother. He joined the family and did his part as a good father should.

XXII. Old Friends Meet

Old friends you've tried and know are true;
'Tis more than can be said of new.

— UNC' BILLY POSSUM

ALREADY PEEPER THE HYLA was singing in the Smiling Pool by night and day, doing his best to tell all the Great World that he was awake and so happy he just couldn't keep still. Peeper is one of those who believe that when you are happy you should tell your neighbors so and try to share your happiness with them.

As he prowled about at night Unc' Billy Possum sometimes would stop to listen to Peeper. When he did he would almost always have a longing to see certain old friends of the summer, friends who had spent the long winter in the Sunny South, the land where Unc' Billy's family had come from and where most of his relatives lived. He wanted to hear about the Sunny South. He wasn't exactly homesick when he heard Peeper singing, but it did give him a queer feeling, a longing for something he couldn't quite name.

Now a number of folk, feathered folk, were already back from the Sunny South. Winsome and Mrs. Bluebird, Welcome and Mrs. Robin, Mr. and Mrs. Phoebe, Little Friend the Song Sparrow and others. Unc' Billy hadn't seen them because he slept while they were awake. He came out only after they had retired for the night. But one night he remained out longer than usual. In fact he remained out all night so that it was broad daylight when he at last decided that it was time for him to retire.

He heard the scream of Redtail the Hawk and that caused him to look up, for he had no desire to furnish a breakfast for Mr. and Mrs. Redtail. Looking up between the bare treetops he saw a great bird sailing high in the sky. At first he thought it was Redtail and prepared to get under cover. Then as he watched the big bird sail in circles with no movement of those broad wings that he could see, suddenly he had that same feeling that the singing of Peeper the Hyla gave him. That wasn't Redtail.

151

No one but his old friend Ol' Mistah Buzzard could sail like that. Ol' Mistah Buzzard was back from the Sunny South! It couldn't be anybody else. No, sir, it couldn't. He had watched Ol' Mistah Buzzard fly too many times not to know him as far as he could see him.

Suddenly he realized that Ol' Mistah Buzzard was coming down. Larger and larger he grew as he descended in a spiral, then finally glided down to land just in front of Unc' Billy.

"Howdy, Brer Possum," said Ol' Mistah Buzzard. "Ah saw yo' from way up yonder and Ah done come down to pass the time of day. What did yo' do through the winter? How is Mis' Possum?"

"Howdy your own self," retorted Unc' Billy. "When did yo'all get back here? Is Mis' Buzzard with yo'? How did yo' leave eve'ybody way down in the Sunny South? Ah reckon yo'all is a bit early gettin' up here; don' yo'all think so?"

"Hol' on, Brer Possum! Hol' on! One question at a time, and anyway mah questions come first," interrupted Ol' Mistah Buzzard.

Unc' Billy grinned. "Ah done sleep all Ah could through the winter and didn't come out 'cepting when Ah just had to have somethin' to eat. Ah haven't seen Mis' Possum lately but Ah reckon she is around somewhere and no worse and no better tempered than usual. Now Ah have answered your questions and it is your turn," said he.

Just then Ol' Mistah Buzzard started to gaze intently up in

the sky. Unc' Billy could see nothing but the sky, but it was clear that Ol' Mistah Buzzard saw more than this. "Ah'll see yo' some other time, Brer Possum," said he as he began to flap his great wings heavily. "Mis' Buzzard is about to arrive and Ah done got to meet her."

He led Mrs. Buzzard down to where Unc' Billy waited.

"Ah suppose Mistress Spring done arrive long ago where yo'all came from," said Unc' Billy.

Mrs. Buzzard nodded. "Leaves all out, flowers all a-blooming and all the feathered folk that gwine to stay there a-nesting right now," said she.

"How come yo'all don' stay down there instead of coming way up here?" inquired Unc' Billy.

"Ah done ask mahself that ve'y thing more than once," replied Mrs. Buzzard. "Ah don' know what we-uns come up here fo' 'cepting fo' a change. Along about this time ev'y year we get right smart anxious fo' a change. Most of our neighbors down there talk about nothin' but getting back no'th. Seem to think they can't nest anywhere but up here. Ah reckon we-uns sort of catch the fever and the first thing we know we-uns are on our way."

"Ah suppose yo'all had plenty of company," said Unc' Billy.

"If yo' mean plenty of feathered folk traveling it is quite true," replied Mrs. Buzzard. "But Ah wouldn't call them company. No, suh, Ah wouldn't call them just that fo' we-uns. You see we-uns done fly high and take it rather easy, just sailin'

153

round and round and keeping our eyes open fo' something to eat. Sometimes some of the Hawk family done travel with us, but we-uns don' care much fo' company. Reckon we-uns got ahead of Mistress Spring some. 'Pears like things haven't started much up here."

"Oh yes they have," replied Unc' Billy promptly. "Ah hear Hooty the Owl done have a couple of babies already and Red-tail the Hawk hasn't wasted any time fo' he and Mrs. Redtail have aiggs Ah am told. Peeper the Hyla is singin' down in the Smiling Pool and Ah can show yo'all some early flowers already. Yes indeed, things have started up here. Yo'all haven't been here long enough to look around. But Ah sho' am glad to see yo'all. Yes, suh, Ah sho' am. Will yo'all build a nest this year?"

Mrs. Buzzard looked at Unc' Billy in disgust. "Since when did yo' ever know we-uns to build a nest?" she asked. "Ah never could see any sense in wasting time that-a-way and Ah haven't changed mah mind now. Ah don't believe in doing things it isn't necessary to do, and the Buzzard family never yet has felt it necessary to build nests. Never could see what Brer Osprey and Brer Redtail and King Eagle and Brer Crow want to build great big nests fo'. Seems foolishment to me. Yes, suh, it seems foolishment to me. Eve'ybody knows just where their aiggs and babies are. Nobody knows where mine are, not if Ah can help it. A big nest way up in a tree looks to me like a lot of work done fo' worse than nothing."

154

Ol' Mistah Buzzard stretched his wings and then held them half lifted so that the air would blow through the feathers. "Ah suppose folks call we-uns lazy," said he, "but Ah don' keer a bit. No, suh, Ah don'. A lot of folks work so much they never have time to enjoy life. Ah may be shiftless but Ah cert'nly knows how to enjoy livin'. We-uns done agree that doing useless things is a waste of time, and we done find out in our family a long time ago that a regular nest isn't needed. So why do a lot of work fo' nothin'?"

To this Unc' Billy had no reply. He was fond of Ol' Mr. Buzzard and Mrs. Buzzard because they were old neighbors, but secretly he thought them lazy. Yes, sir, he thought them lazy. They didn't build a nest. They didn't even catch their food, but lived on what they could find that others had left.

"Lazy," thought Unc' Billy. "That is what they are — lazy. But they cert'nly do seem to enjoy life."

XXIII. Little Mrs. Timmy Moves

To self a mother gives no thought
When babies are in peril caught.
— OLD MOTHER NATURE

IN THE GREEN FOREST and on the Green Meadows
mothers, big and little, are good mothers. At least this is true
of most of them. Of course there are some who have no real
mother love. There are the Turtle folk and the Fish folk and
the Frog folk and the Toad folk. Most of these never even know
their own children. But as a rule among the little folk in fur and

feathers mother love is very strong. It is so strong that at times the smallest and most timid become wonderfully brave.

A little way in from the edge of the Green Forest and directly above the Crooked Little Path was the home of Timmy the Flying Squirrel. Perhaps I should say the home of Mrs. Timmy, for just at this time Timmy was living elsewhere. You see there were five babies in that snug home so of course there was no room for Timmy.

It was a very comfortable home. It was in a hollow in a big limb high up in a tree. Drummer the Woodpecker had cut out that home. Rather, he and Mrs. Drummer, working together, had cut it out. They had raised a family in it and then gone away. Timmy and Mrs. Timmy had moved in. They had made a soft and very comfortable bed. Mrs. Timmy felt that it was the nicest and safest home she had ever had for helpless babies. No one excepting Timmy ever visited it. From the little round doorway she could look out and see for quite a distance in the dusk of early evening and in the moonlight.

Now there are few little people more timid than the Flying Squirrels. They are gentle little folk who have learned that there are fewer enemies in the night than during the day. So it is seldom that they come out in daytime unless it happens that the day is dull and dark. But with the coming of dusk they are out sailing from tree to tree, hunting for food and having a wonderful time. Then they have little fear of anyone save a member of the Owl family.

With the arrival of the five babies Mrs. Timmy became, like all mothers, anxious every minute she was away from them. She was constantly on the watch for enemies. Things of which she had no fear for herself worried her on account of the babies. So it was that when one day Farmer Brown's boy happened to stop at the foot of that tree and rap on it, just to see if there might be a bird nesting in that hole which he could see, Mrs. Timmy popped her head out to see what the cause of the noise was. Farmer Brown's boy saw her and she saw Farmer Brown's boy. He guessed right away that probably there were babies up there, but he had no intention of disturbing them.

Of course Mrs. Timmy didn't know this. Had she had no babies she probably wouldn't have thought of leaving the home. Having babies, she at once became alarmed. What if that two-legged creature should try to get her babies. She made a long flying leap from her doorway, gliding down to the foot of a tree fifty feet away. Up this she ran swiftly and, leaping from the top, glided down to the foot of another tree still farther away. She hoped Farmer Brown's boy would follow her. He didn't.

"Oh dear!" thought Mrs. Timmy. "What shall I do now? He may climb up there and get my babies. I don't know what to do. They are not safe there any more. No, sir, they are not safe. I never shall rest easy now that two-legged creature knows where my home is."

She watched Farmer Brown's boy go off whistling on his way

home. She heard his whistle grow fainter and fainter as he got farther and farther away. Finally it ceased altogether. Farmer Brown's boy had left the Green Forest. Behind him he had left Mrs. Timmy and in her heart he had left fear. He didn't know it. He wouldn't have done it for the world could he have helped it.

Mrs. Timmy was worried. Yes, sir, Mrs. Timmy was worried. "Now that that two-legged creature knows where we are living I'll never know another minute of peace here," said Mrs. Timmy to herself. "My babies are safe only when no one knows where they are. I must get them out of here. I must find a new home for them."

Although it was in the daytime, and Mrs. Timmy does not like to be out in the daylight, she went straight over to another tree some distance away, a tree she knew all about. High up in this tree was another old home of Drummer the Woodpecker. She knew all about it. That is, she had known all about it. The only thing she didn't know about it now was whether or not it was being used by someone else. She went over to investigate. Cautiously she poked her head into the entrance. There was no one in there. There was, however, a nest in there. It was an old nest that had been built in there the year before by a pair of Bluebirds.

"Good," said Mrs. Timmy to herself. "This bed will do for the present. I can move the children first and then move the bed afterward. It may not be necessary to move at all but I'll feel easier if we do move. I'll feel easier for knowing that that two-legged creature doesn't know where we are. Supposing he should take a notion to want one of my babies!" Little Mrs. Timmy shuddered at the thought.

She went back home. For a few moments she sat looking out of her doorway. She was making sure that no one was watching. Then she went in the house and a moment later she was back in that doorway carrying one of her babies. She had hold of him by the skin of his breast and his arms and legs were curled up around her neck. She carried him up to the top of the tree. Then she made a long leap out into space. Spreading her arms and legs out as far as possible, so that the flap of skin between wrist and ankle on each side was stretched out flat, she glided down, down, down to the foot of another tree fifty feet away. As she approached this she glided up slightly and alighted gently on the trunk, still holding her baby. Up this tree she ran to jump again and glide to another tree. A third time she did it and this brought her to the tree where her new home was to be. The baby was placed in the nest and mother returned. This time she did not follow the same route. She made one jump of a hundred feet. You see, with no baby to carry she could jump and glide farther. Flying Squirrels do not fly; they glide.

So, one by one, the five babies were carried by that wonderful little mother to the new home, and not once did she go down on

the ground. Then when the last one was safely in the new home she once more returned to the old home. This time she got a big mouthful of the soft bedding there and carried that to the new home and tucked it in and around and under the babies. Back again for more bedding, and back again, until at last all of it had been carried over to the new home. Then, and then only, did that wonderful little mother draw a long breath free of anxiety.

XXIV. The Unjust Neighbors

When shines the sun some folks want rain;
But when it pours they still complain.

— STICKYTOES

IT WAS CLEAR WEATHER. It had been clear weather for some time. Every day jolly, round, bright Mr. Sun climbed up in the blue, blue sky and smiled his broadest. It was hot. It was very hot. After a time people began to complain. The ground became very, very dry. The plants became very, very thirsty. Even the trees, though their roots went deep in the ground, could not find moisture enough, and their leaves began to droop.

Stickytoes, the Tree Toad, like the other members of the Frog and Toad families, needs a moist skin. He is most uncomfortable if his skin becomes dry. Indeed, it makes him sick. So Stickytoes was reasonably comfortable only at night when jolly, round bright Mr. Sun had gone to bed behind the Purple Hills. During the day he remained quiet in the coolest place he could find, a little hollow in his home tree. He was quite out of sight there so that the feathered folk who occasionally visited that tree never saw him.

But Stickytoes saw them and he heard them. Even when he couldn't see them he could hear them and what he heard was just one long string of complaints.

"I don't see what Old Mother Nature is thinking of not to send up a rain cloud," said Sammy Jay.

"If it doesn't rain soon we are going to have trouble to find enough to eat," said Welcome Robin. "I haven't had an earthworm for so long that I have almost forgotten what it looks like. The ground is baked so hard that no worms ever come to the top. Fruit is drying up."

"Laughing Brook isn't laughing any more," reported Blacky the Crow. "There are just little pools. I don't know what is going to become of us."

Stickytoes himself said nothing. He listened to the complaints of others but he kept his own mouth tightly closed. Not so much as a peep did he utter, yet probably there was not one of those who were complaining who was quite as uncomfortable as was he. Every day it grew worse. Then one day he heard someone asking where he was and saying that he should be found and made to call rain.

"If Stickytoes calls for rain, rain will come," said the voice. "I've seen it happen over and over again."

"I have too," said another voice. "Anyone who can call rain and doesn't at a time like this should be made to suffer."

"They ought to know better," said Stickytoes to himself. "Yes, sir, they ought to know better. They have short memories. I've been blamed this way before and it is most unjust. I can call for rain but I can't call rain. Calling has nothing whatever to do with bringing the rain. They ought to know it. They just don't stop to think. If they did they would know that when I call I am doing it because I know that rain is coming. I can feel it coming. I suppose I feel it sooner than others do and when I do feel it it makes me feel so good that I just have to tell everybody else."

You know how it is when gossip gets well started. It just travels everywhere fast, and it has little regard for truth. So it was that the gossip about Stickytoes and his calling of rain traveled fast and far and wide, and there was a great deal of talk about it. Whereas at first he had kept out of sight to avoid the heat, he now stayed there to avoid being seen by his neighbors because he realized that they were becoming more and more angry with him, and all because of a silly story that he could call rain.

"Just as if I wouldn't call it if I could," said Stickytoes to himself. "Not one of them wants rain any more than I do. I doubt if any one of them wants it as much as I do. I never felt worse in my life. Wouldn't I be silly not to call rain if I could? This is a funny world. A lot of people believe what they want to believe,

169

even though there be no truth in it, and all the talking in the world won't make them believe anything else."

Do you wonder that Stickytoes felt that his neighbors were most unjust? Of course he had nothing to do with the weather. You see, it had happened in summers past that after a long dry spell the voice of Stickytoes had been heard and very soon rain had fallen. The reason for this was that Stickytoes' skin is very, very sensitive and when there is the least bit of moisture in the air he feels it. So, before the coming of a storm he will feel the first bit of moisture in the air before anyone else can detect any sign of it. Then he knows the rain is coming and he expresses his joy by calling.

The trouble with a great many people is that, having knowledge, they do not make use of it. They do not use their memories. So they make hasty decisions which, had they really stopped to think, they never would have made.

Blacky the Crow is accounted one of the smartest and wisest of all the feathered folk. In fact he is considered one of the smartest of all the people in the Green Forest or on the Green Meadows. The reason for this is that Blacky has a good memory and never fails to use it. He doesn't jump to conclusions. He goes back in his memory for all the facts that he has ever learned about any subject. You know, one's memory is a sort of storehouse. Of course if you don't use your storehouse it is useless. Blacky uses his.

He heard all the gossip about Stickytoes and his supposed

ability to call rain. For a while he said nothing. Then, as some of the other people became more and more insistent that Stickytoes should be found and made to call rain, Blacky spoke his mind.

"You are just wasting your time," said he. "All of you are most unjust to a good neighbor. I remember a drouth just as bad as this. I remember the neighbors getting just as excited about it as you are now, and blaming Stickytoes just as you are doing. Stickytoes had nothing to do with that dry weather. But I found out then that Stickytoes himself can tell long before any of the rest of us can when rain is coming. When you hear his voice he is not calling for rain, but is telling us all that he knows that rain will come soon. How he knows, I don't know, but I do know that he does know. So if you'll take my advice you'll go about your business and forget Stickytoes until you hear him."

So Blacky went about his business and took no part in the foolish hunt for Stickytoes. Always he had his ears open for the voice of Stickytoes, but otherwise he gave the matter no further thought. Down inside, he laughed at the silliness of his neighbors. "I hope," said he to himself, "that Stickytoes keeps well hidden. It will be just too bad if some of these silly folks should find him and do him harm."

"It isn't fair. It isn't fair at all," said Stickytoes over and over to himself. "When I feel the first sign of rain I am always glad to tell whoever will listen. It has always been so. This time, however, I have a mind to keep still. It would serve them right. They ought to be made to wait until the very last minute."

Down in his heart Stickytoes knew that he wouldn't wait. He knew that he couldn't wait. He knew that, with the first hint of coming rain, he would be so bursting with joy that he just couldn't keep still. The heat increased. The pastures grew brown. The leaves hung limp on the trees and some yellowed and fell. In the Green Forest there was a great fear, the fear of the Red Terror, which is fire. That always is the most dreadful of all the dangers which come with dry weather.

Then on a day that to others seemed as hot and dry as ever, Stickytoes felt a change. Rain was on the way. He began to call. "Rain is coming. Rain is coming," he called. It did come the very next day.

XXV. Mrs. Whitefoot Seeks A Change

Make up your mind, then never doubt
You know just what you are about.

— MRS. WHITEFOOT

WHITEFOOT THE WOOD MOUSE and Mrs. Whitefoot had lived all summer under an old stump near the edge of the Green Forest. Now the children had gone out into the Great World and Whitefoot and his pretty little mate had no more worries on their account.

Whitefoot was fond of that old stump. He liked to climb up on it and sit there while he made his toilet. He was very particular about his appearance. He was careful that there should be no spots on his fawn-colored coat and his white waistcoat. He took the greatest care of his white feet and hands. The top of that old stump was a lovely place to sit while he washed them, using his tongue for a washcloth after the manner of Black Pussy.

In a hollow in that stump was a precious store of seeds which he and Mrs. Whitefoot had thriftily gathered for winter use. They are among the little wise folk who look ahead.

"My dear," said Whitefoot in his small squeaky voice, "I think this is the best home we've ever had."

"Do you?" replied Mrs. Whitefoot.

"Don't you?" demanded Whitefoot.

"It has been a very good home for the summer, but now that cold weather is here I am wondering if it isn't time for a change," squeaked Mrs. Whitefoot.

Whitefoot turned with a look of startled surprise in his soft eyes. "Time for a change!" he squeaked. "Why should we change? Why should we think of changing? What is the matter with this home? Where will we find a better one? Tell me that."

"That is what we will have to find out," replied Mrs. Whitefoot mildly.

"But what is the matter with our home here? Tell me one single thing that is wrong," persisted Whitefoot.

"Too many folks know where we live," retorted Mrs. White-foot. "No one can live in one place as long as we have lived here and keep it a secret."

"So what?" squeaked Whitefoot impatiently.

"So sooner or later someone with a liking for fat Mice — and you are fat — is going to watch this home of ours to give one of us a surprise, an unpleasant surprise," declared Mrs. Whitefoot.

"Such as?" squeaked Whitefoot in an inquiring tone.

"Spooky the Screech Owl or his big cousin, Hooty the Great Horned Owl, Black Pussy the Cat, or Reddy Fox, or — "

"Never mind any more," Whitefoot interrupted hastily. "You don't *know* that any of those folks will be watching for us."

"And I don't know that they *won't* be. I like to know that such a thing *won't* happen, not that it *can* happen," squeaked Mrs. Whitefoot.

"So what?" demanded Whitefoot again.

"So it is time for a change and I am going to look around," replied little Mrs. Whitefoot in such a decided tone that White-foot knew it would be useless to argue. It is surprising how decided a small person can be.

"Whoo, hoo, hoo, hoo!" called Hooty the Owl from behind them.

"You are right, my dear, it is time for a change," squeaked Whitefoot as they darted inside that hollow old stump.

So every night Mrs. Whitefoot went house hunting, and because he disliked being left alone, or was afraid she wouldn't come back, Whitefoot went along. Mrs. Whitefoot was hard to suit. Anyway that is what Whitefoot thought. He made the mistake of saying so. "So I am hard to suit," squeaked Mrs. Whitefoot sharply. "Well, it is a good thing that I am. If I wasn't goodness knows what would become of us. I don't want even to think of what might happen to us if we were to move into any of the places you have thought good enough. They may be good enough, but they are not safe enough. I know what I want and I shall keep looking until I find it. I haven't seen anything yet that suits me."

"I dislike to say it, my dear, but you are too fussy," said Whitefoot.

"So you think I'm fussy!" cried Mrs. Whitefoot and her voice was squeakier than ever. "I'm not fussy. I have no patience with fussy people, so don't you dare to call me fussy. Refusing something you don't want when you know what you do want isn't fussiness. Every place we have looked at is just the sort of place that other folks would expect Wood Mice to live in. I want a place that no one would think of looking in for a Mouse and I am going to find it."

Whitefoot had a sharp retort on the end of his tongue but he kept it there. He heard the rustle of leaves as Mrs. Whitefoot scampered away. He didn't run after her as he usually did. He climbed up on the end of a log and sulked and while he sulked he washed his tail. Soon he forgot to sulk. It always is difficult to do two things at once. So when you feel sulky get busy doing something. It is a sure cure for sulkiness.

Presently Mrs. Whitefoot returned. She was excited. "Follow me!" she squeaked and darted away. Whitefoot ran after her. She led him to the edge of the Green Forest where the Crooked Little Path begins. She stopped beneath a small tree. "Look up over your head!" she squeaked excitedly. Whitefoot looked up. He didn't see anything to get excited about. All he saw was the big gray former home of Madam Baldface the Wasp.

Looking up at that big gray house high above him he couldn't believe that Mrs. Whitefoot could really mean she was interested in that. He thought she must be joking.

"I don't see anything that looks like a new home for us," he squeaked.

"Don't you see that big gray house up there?" demanded Mrs. Whitefoot.

"Of course I see it. That's the home of Madam Baldface and her hot-tempered children," squeaked Whitefoot.

"You mean *was* their home. It is ours now," replied Mrs. Whitefoot.

Whitefoot stared at his pretty little mate. "Are you crazy?" he demanded.

"Not a bit. Just clever," replied Mrs. Whitefoot with a squeaky little chuckle.

"Are you telling me that you think we are going to live way

177

up there in that thing?" cried Whitefoot, and his voice was squeakier than ever.

Now what was way up to Whitefoot really wasn't high at all. Some folks in the Green Forest would have called it low. It was because he is himself such a small person that Whitefoot thought that house was high up.

"That is where we are going to live. That is our new home or will be when we move in," said Mrs. Whitefoot.

"Now I know you're crazy! Whoever heard of any of our folks living in such a place as that?" cried Whitefoot.

"I have heard that it has been done. Now we are going to try it ourselves. We've lived in an old nest of one of our feathered neighbors just as high up as that is. We had to roof it over ourselves. Now here is a house all roofed over. All we have to do is to make a comfortable bed inside and move in. It will be everything that a Mouse home should be," declared little Mrs. Whitefoot.

"A home should be safe," squeaked Whitefoot. "That doesn't look warm enough or strong enough. We need a warm house in winter. I can't sleep when I'm cold. And that looks to me as if rough Brother North Wind is likely to tear it to pieces the first time he tries."

"You just don't know what you are talking about," squeaked Mrs. Whitefoot sharply. "That house up there will be our new home, so make up your mind to that and like it. Now come up and see what it is like inside." She led the way and Whitefoot followed.

XXVI. A Castle in the Air

If you find your stand is wrong,
Then quit it.
If you find you err at all,
Admit it.

— **WHITEFOOT**

WHITEFOOT FOLLOWED Mrs. Whitefoot up to the big gray house that Madam Baldface the Wasp and her children had built in the summer but no longer used. It hung from a branch near the end of a limb of a young tree and was just high enough above the ground to be out of reach of Reddy Fox even though he jumped as high as he could. To anyone as small as a

Mouse that was very high indeed. When he had climbed up to it Whitefoot felt as if he were way up in the sky.

Mrs. Whitefoot had already made an entrance just big enough to slip through comfortably and had torn out some of the paper comb which had pretty well filled the inside of that big house. The comb, you know, is made up of the little cells in which the baby Wasps are born. It is like the honeycomb of a Honeybee only made of paper instead of wax. There was a lot of it, for Madam Baldface had had a big family.

"We'll clean all this out and then we will make a nice nest in here and we will have the most wonderful house we ever have had," declared Mrs. Whitefoot. She was excited and full of enthusiasm. It was catching. In spite of himself Whitefoot began to take a lively interest. Being honest he grudgingly admitted that it might do.

"It is warmer in here than I thought it would be," said Whitefoot.

"It will be warmer still when we have our nest made," declared Mrs. Whitefoot. "Rough Brother North Wind can't get in here if he tries. Have you noticed how dry it is? There is no leak anywhere. No matter how hard a storm may be we will be snug and warm and dry. Isn't it wonderful?"

Whitefoot had been examining the entrance and had been surprised at the thickness of the wall. It wasn't just one thickness of that gray material which really is a kind of paper, for you know the Wasps found out how to make paper long, long, long before Man did. It was made of several layers. That is what made that house so warm and dry and also so strong.

"I wouldn't have believed it!" said Whitefoot.

"What wouldn't you have believed?" asked Mrs. Whitefoot.

"That I would ever even think of living in a house made by Madam Baldface and her children," replied Whitefoot.

"There is one thing we must never forget," said Mrs. Whitefoot as she poked her nose out of the little round doorway, then hastily withdrew it.

"What is that?" Whitefoot wanted to know.

"We must make as sure as we can that no one ever sees us climbing up and down. If no one ever sees us doing that no one will ever think of looking here for us," replied Mrs. Whitefoot.

"Is that why you drew back just now?" asked Whitefoot.

Mrs. Whitefoot nodded. "I saw a shadow moving," said she.

"Pooh! What's a shadow?" squeaked Whitefoot.

"It might be Spooky the Screech Owl or his big cousin, Hooty," replied Mrs. Whitefoot severely.

"Of course you are right, my dear, as you usually are," agreed Whitefoot meekly. "We can't be too careful, especially on a night like this. Mistress Moon never has been brighter."

Mrs. Whitefoot was peeping outside again. Whitefoot joined her. Outside it was almost as light as day. A big shadow moved across an opening below. They recognized that shadow. They had seen it too often before. Then they saw the maker of it, Hooty the Owl. He stopped on top of a tall stub of a tree and stood so still and straight that he looked like a part of it. Had they not seen him light there they might not have seen him at all.

"He is watching our old home under that old stump. He knows where we lived and he doesn't know we have moved. I told you it was time we got a new home," whispered Mrs. Whitefoot.

For a long time Hooty sat without moving, watching the hole under the stump that was the doorway to their old home. Finally he gave up and flew away. Hardly had he disappeared when along the Crooked Little Path came Reddy Fox. Very handsome he looked in the moonlight. He was walking lightly. Not a leaf rustled. His black ears were cocked to catch the faintest sound. He lifted his head to test the air with his wonderful nose. The black shadows had gathered just back of the old stump. Reddy stepped into their midst and sat down. He was within an easy jump of the hole under the stump. Whitefoot nudged Mrs. Whitefoot. She nudged him back. They watched the watcher. Were they glad they had moved when they did? What do you think?

After Reddy left Whitefoot was ready to go look for his dinner, but he sat in the doorway for another good look around. He looked down the Crooked Little Path. He looked up the Crooked Little Path. He looked on both sides of the Crooked Little Path. He looked once more up the Crooked Little Path.

Then for an instant Whitefoot held his breath. He tried not

to believe he saw what his eyes told him he did see. In the moonlight, running down the Crooked Little Path, was a slim, trim, small person dressed all in white save for the black end of his tail. It was his winter coat. He was no bigger around than Whitefoot, if as big, but he was nearly twice as long. It was Little Terror, as some of the smaller Green Forest folk call Shadow the Weasel. He is the one person among all the folk who live in the Green Forest whom the smaller folk most fear.

Just seeing him running along in the moonlight made White-foot shake as if he had chills. He shook with fright, not cold. Mrs. Whitefoot joined him and peeped out. She also shook. From big enemies they might escape by hiding in places too small for enemies to follow, but from Little Terror there was no such hiding place. Where they could go he could go.

They watched him now as he turned aside to examine the old stump under which they had lived all summer and in which was their storehouse filled with seeds. He climbed up on the old stump. He disappeared inside. The two Wood Mice looked at each other and knew that each was thinking the same thing. Supposing one of them had been in there! They shivered more than ever.

Little Terror was out now. Nimbly he ran down the old stump and began to look around the base of it. He found the entrance to their old house, a hole between two roots. It was just big enough for them to go through with comfort. Little Terror disappeared inside. When he came out his eyes were red with rage because of disappointment. He stopped right under the gray Wasp's house and looked up at it. Of course he couldn't see into it and that was a very good thing for the two frightened little folk looking down at him. They held their breath as they watched him. Would he climb that tree to investigate? If he did what could they do? Nothing. There was nothing at all that they could do. For only a moment those little red eyes glared up. It was the longest moment those frightened little folk had ever known. Anyway it seemed so.

"Nothing there to interest me. Wonder where those hot-tempered folks who made that thing are this cold weather. Probably they are inside there. They can stay there for all I care," thought the Weasel and left the neighborhood. The two little watchers could see him for some distance because against the brown carpet of fallen leaves his white coat made it easy for eyes to follow. It would have been just the other way had snow covered the ground.

"If we had still been living in our old home under the stump —" began Mrs. Whitefoot. She didn't finish because Whitefoot interrupted.

"But we were not, thanks to you, my dear!" he cried happily.

The Crooked Little Path shows the way through the Green Forest. If you be light of foot, keen of eye and ear, quick of understanding and soft-spoken, it will lead you to pleasant adventures in happy living.